MW01223085

Encounters With Life
Tales Of Living, Loving, & Laughter
James Osborne

Encounters With Life

Tales of

Living, Loving & Laughter

James Osborne

To Michael
Best Wishes!
James O
March 2020

Encounters With Life

Tales of

Living, Loving & Laughter

James Osborne

Cover Art:
Michelle Crocker
www.mlcdesigns4you.com

Publisher's Note:

This is a work of fiction. All names, characters, places, and events are the work of the author's imagination.

Any resemblance to real persons, places, or events is coincidental.

Solstice Publishing - www.solsticepublishing.com

For Sharolie
whose encouragement was instrumental
in the writing and assembling of this collection

and

For our children and grandchildren
who make it all worthwhile

Contents

Dragonflies and The Great Blue Heron

For more than a decade, Great Blue Herons had a special meaning for Jim and Judi. During those years, Jim had no hint their affection for these graceful birds would one day take on a much deeper significance.

The couple enjoyed watching them from the deck of their summer cottage on the shores of Kootenay Lake, nestled in the mountains of southeastern British Columbia. The tall birds would hunt for food less than 200 feet away, drawn by schools of minnows to a small bay screened by willows from their deck above.

Jim and Judi could also watch the long-legged birds fish patiently in the reedy shallows of a sheltered cove where they often anchored their boat overnight. Blue heron became their mascot. Thus, it was fitting to celebrate their 30th wedding anniversary by commissioning a watercolor of a nesting pair.

And then the years slipped by, as they will. Those 30 years edged toward 35. Their prized painting hadn't been framed. One day, Jim snuck the rolled up watercolor out of their house and got it framed. On the night of their 35th anniversary, as they prepared to turn in for the night, there was the framed painting, above their bed where Jim had just finished hanging it minutes earlier.

Three years later, Judi lost a 13-month battle with cancer. And Jim was, well... lost, too.

At Judi's memorial service, a dear friend and former colleague led the service. In her remarks, Eva was determined to help Judi's young grandchildren and other children among the large assembly of mourners comprehend what was occurring.

Eva told this brilliant story:

Once upon a time, a happy group of tiny bugs was

playing on the bottom of a lily pond. One by one, the bugs began climbing up a lily stem and disappearing. Those left behind wondered what had happened to their friends. Then they agreed the next bug to venture beyond the surface of the pond would return and tell the others what they'd experienced.

One day, a bug left and found itself on a lily pad. It fell asleep. When it awoke, the warm sunshine had dried its body. Instinctively, it spread the wings that it had grown while asleep and began flying away. The bug had become a beautiful dragonfly with four iridescent wings. Then it remembered the promise. It swooped back toward the surface of the pond and headed downward. The dragonfly hit the surface and could go no farther. It was not able to return. After a while, it finally realized the others would just need to have faith that it was going to be all right.

Before she died, Judi had asked Jim to make two promises: to live a healthy lifestyle, and to find someone with whom to spend the rest of his life. The first was easy. He struggled with the second. It was shelved for almost three years. Then he met Sharolie.

Soon, it was obvious Sharolie was an extraordinary woman, just as Judi had been. Sharolie understood Jim's still-raw grief. She encouraged him to talk about the experiences of the 38 years that he and Judi had shared together. Sharolie said it helped her to know and understand both of them better. Like Judi, Sharolie was blessed with a generous nature. Both had the capacity to recognize in others virtues that many others might overlook, ignore, miss or fear.

One day, Sharolie's instincts and deep spirituality drew her to visit a yoga ashram near Jim's place on the lake. Jim went along, partly out of curiosity but mostly to be with her. After all, they were still immersed in the euphoria of newfound love.

It was early afternoon and sunny when Jim and

Sharolie arrived at the picturesque ashram overlooking Kootenay Lake. They parked their car at the main building. The two walked along a narrow winding path through dense trees, over a footbridge and across lawns toward their destination, a domed temple, the centerpiece of the ashram.

Suddenly, a large shadow crossed their path. They heard a rush of wings overhead. Both Jim and Sharolie looked up. A Great Blue Heron had swept low over them, then folded its six-foot wingspan and landed 75 feet away in a vegetable garden, on the far side of a tall fence. A few steps beyond the blue heron, four people were busy tilling and harvesting in the garden. The big majestic bird took no notice of them. It was unusual behavior for the famously shy blue herons.

Sharolie and Jim were in awe as they savored the experience. Each found themselves exchanging meaningful looks with the blue heron. It took several minutes to pull themselves away. Full of questions, they continued on to the temple. Half an hour passed while they enjoyed the temple's extraordinary acoustics and ambiance. Then it was time to go.

The couple emerged from the ground-level main entrance to another startling surprise. A blue heron was standing in the middle of a 30-foot circular lily pond, centerpiece of the main entrance. Like the earlier blue heron, the five-foot bird was staring right at them, calmly and unblinking. Could it be the same one they'd seen earlier? Jim and Sharolie were sure it was. If the first encounter was unusual, this one had to be exceptional. More was to come.

Enthralled, the couple watched the stately blue-gray bird for several more minutes, unwilling to break the spell. While they stood transfixed, numerous other visitors walked by, to and from the temple, glancing over their shoulders at the rare sight. Again, the blue heron paid no attention to those passing by. Patiently and unblinking, it returned Sharolie and Jim's amazed gazes.

"It has to be a message," Sharolie whispered quietly. "It has to be from Judi. It just has to be! The heron is bringing a message from her. I just know it."

Eventually, the couple walked slowly a few feet along the main sidewalk away from the lily pond. They turned back. The blue heron was still there, still watching them. Again, it returned their gazes. Then Jim and Sharolie finally turned and made their way along a secondary walk beside the temple to a cliff overlooking the lake. While enjoying the spectacular view, they were unable to wrest their minds away from the lily pond, now hidden from view. They headed back.

"I wonder," Jim said. "Do you think it's still there?" He was skeptical of Sharolie's assessment of their experience. Sharolie's face displayed a matter-of-fact look of silent confidence that spoke wordlessly, 'of course'.

Sure enough, the blue heron was still there. Once again, it quietly returned their gazes. This was uncanny, they both agreed. After several more disquieting minutes, Jim and Sharolie reluctantly pulled themselves away from the blue heron and the lily pond, and returned back down the path though the grove of trees to their car. Both wondered how long the blue heron might have remained there, had they stayed. They marveled at the rare behavior of the blue heron.

"Yes... I'm sure," Sharolie kept repeating. "I'm sure. That was Judi sending you a message... sending us a message... telling you it's okay now. I think Judi's saying she knows you've kept your second promise. She's going to be okay now."

Jim and Sharolie didn't know at the time that the blue heron episodes would be just one part of their love story.

After Jim and Sharolie met, he wanted his three

daughters to share his joy at having found someone who he knew Judi would happily endorse. The first daughter to meet Sharolie was Kim. She invited her Dad and Sharolie to a semi-pro baseball game.

The three adults and Kim's children had settled in to watch the game from the open-air stands. Suddenly, two enormous dragonflies swept around Sharolie and settled calmly on the baseball hat she was wearing.

"Oh, my God!" Kim screamed, jumping to her feet. "Look at that! Look! Dragonflies! Two of them! Oh my God! Oh my God! You know what that means, don't you?"

In her mind, Eva's parable of the dragonflies had come true. From that day forward, no one was going to dissuade Kim from believing those dragonflies were on a mission of approval from her late Mother.

Since then, Jim and Sharolie have experienced hovering dragonflies, often in the most unlikely locations. And they continued to encounter blue herons, time and time again. Like the dragonflies, these encounters were often in unusual and unexpected circumstances. Close friends also reported sightings of blue herons, unusually close up and where they'd never seen them before.

Jim and Sharolie were married 23 months after they met. Shortly thereafter, the visits from the blue heron and dragonflies began to diminish.

Now, the visits are less frequent although always welcome.

On those occasions, Sharolie will say, "Checking up. She's just checking up."

Source Credit: Eva's dragonfly analogy is drawn from a public domain story, "The Water Bug Story", at www.healingheart.net/stories/waterbug.html

Boat Rides and Bearskins

For years, Tom and Susan dreamed of owning a boat like this. Their sleek 25-foot boat had arrived in late summer. They could sleep and cook on board. It even had a toilet, or 'head' as sailors call it. And as expected, it brought many unforgettable experiences... including one that almost cost them their lives.

The scene was Kootenay Lake. The long picturesque lake runs for 70 miles between mountain ranges. It offers a tantalizing choice of bays to explore, many with secluded sandy beaches surrounded by spectacular scenery.

Tom and Susan spent the last months of their first season learning the basics of handling their big new boat. One especially tricky challenge was navigating a narrow passage in and out of the marina where they moored the boat. Originally built for smaller boats, the entrance required precise navigation. Both sides of the tight L-shaped entry were made of massive boulders piled high. The design protected the marina from violent storms known to frequent Kootenay Lake. Fellow boaters in the marina warned them about the storms; fierce winds and enormous waves can come up without warning within seconds.

When the following summer finally arrived, Tom and Susan set out immediately touring the lake's sparkling blue waters, often anchoring overnight in little bays accessible only by boat. One of their favorites was a narrow cove with a sandy beach protected on both sides by 30-foot high rocky outcroppings. The still-novice boaters felt almost as secure in that bay as in their marina, 15 miles north on the opposite side of the four-mile-wide lake.

One evening they were enjoying a campfire on the cove's crescent-shaped beach. The cloudless sky promised a carpet of stars that night, with no moon to interfere.

Without warning, just before dusk they heard an

outboard motor. A small aluminum boat carrying a dark shape appeared around a rock outcropping at the head of the bay. Tom and Susan heard the motor slow almost to an idle. It was heading straight for them.

Seated in the aluminum boat was a dark and strange looking figure, a rifle clutched in one hand and the tiller in the other. A black stovepipe hat perched atop his head. It failed to tame the dark figure's long scraggly shoulder-length hair. The wide brim made it look ominous... like a witch's hat. The rest of the figure looked even more bizarre. An unruly black beard announced him to be male. His jacket and pants were of scraped bearskin like those of backwoods mountain men. The hat was made of some other hide, perhaps shaved beaver.

Tom and Susan watched apprehensively as the boat scraped to a stop on the rough sand of the beach, too close for comfort. The man removed his hat, scratched his head and beard, and then glared at the couple.

"Good evening," Tom said.

The stranger ignored him still clutching the rifle. A fishing rod poked up over one side of the 17-foot boat. Sticking up from the bow, Tom and Susan spotted a sharp fishing gaff. Its curved razor sharp hook did nothing to ease their tension.

The man stepped nimbly over the side into six inches of water, revealing knee-high boots also made from some kind of animal hide. He pulled the boat far up onto the beach, tying it to a stout tree. He began walking toward them, the rifle held at alert in his right hand and the fishing rod draped over his opposite shoulder.

Tom and Susan each silently thought about defensive weapons. She tried to gauge her distance to a pile of dead tree branches they'd gathered for firewood. He reached behind his back and loosened the clasp of a hunting knife sheath on his belt.

"How're ya doin'?" the man said, stopping ten feet

from the campfire. His voice was gruff and emotionless.

"Ah, just fine," the nervous couple replied together.

"How about you?" Tom added.

"Been fishin", the stranger answered, gesturing with the fishing rod. He shifted the rifle onto his shoulder. "No luck."

The man turned to go and then stopped: "Mind if my wife and I join your campfire?"

Tom and Susan glanced at each other surprised, silently asking themselves, 'wife?' This wild man didn't look to be the married type.

"Sure," they said together again, uncertain about what that meant.

"Camped over the ridge," the man said, pointing up a heavily treed slope beyond the beach.

His comment startled Tom and Susan. They'd visited the cove a few times. As usual, the two had gone exploring after setting up their camp. They'd encountered no other campsites, and would have seen anyone arriving. The beach was accessible only by boat. What if it wasn't true that he was married? The uncertainty added to their unease. What's more, they'd gone skinny dipping after setting up camp. So the area wasn't private after all. Susan was more than a little uncomfortable.

"Back in a bit," the man said abruptly and turned away. He disappeared into the gloom beyond the light of the campfire, leaving in his wake a distinctive smell of bear grease mingled with the acrid odor of sweat.

Tom and Susan looked at each other, silently knowing they'd prefer to never see him again. They wondered apprehensively where in the darkness he'd gone. Did he go where he said, or was he circling around them for some nefarious reason? They weren't sure; they discussed potential defensive maneuvers and escape routes, just in case. Susan found a stout piece of firewood and put it beside her chair. Tom checked his hunting knife and positioned a sharp metal wiener stick beside him.

Within minutes it was totally dark. The moonless night deepened their unease. They forgot about the stars. Tom piled more wood on the campfire. Susan sat huddled in a beach chair, pulling her warm coat tighter around her petite frame.

A half-hour later they were startled when a female voice behind them called out from the dark:

“Hi there. May we join you?”

Good grammar, Tom thought, his mind seeking reassurance and finding a tincture of humor in the irony.

“Of course,” Tom replied, sounding more confident than he felt as he and Susan stood. “Welcome!”

A sturdy middle-aged woman dressed in a bright print sarong walked into the light of the campfire. She wore a grey knit shawl over her shoulders. The woman’s face bore a pleasant, relaxed smile... her eyes genuinely friendly. Behind her was the man they’d seen earlier, now hatless. He stepped forward into the light, a hint of a smile creeping out from behind his long bushy beard. The man had on a hand-woven cotton shirt with red, brown and grey vertical stripes. Over it was a hand-made leather vest. The neck of the collarless shirt and the cuffs were tightly buttoned. His long dark hair was combed now and kept under control by a rough-hewn leather headband tied behind with rawhide laces.

The visitors initiated the introductions. Claire explained she was a loans manager for a bank in the small city a few miles south of the lake. Her husband Andrew was a ‘free spirit’, she said. Andrew sat without speaking on a log beside her, looking content as she carried the conversation. Claire told them Andrew worked for the government, grooming hiking trails in parks when not teaching outdoor survival skills.

The unusual couple turned out to be a fascinating dichotomy of town and country lifestyles. Tom and Susan were enthralled further as they listened to their visitors' stories, particularly Clair's version of Andrew's lifestyle. During one of the few times he did participate in the conversation, Andrew said he was committed to living in an environmentally respectful way, following as much as possible a 19th Century way of living. When the visit ended, Claire invited Tom and Susan to visit their camp the following day.

The next morning they made their way up from the beach along a faint path through brush and trees to the ridge. There in a dense grove of trees they found a large A-frame tent made from bear hides. The tent floor was also made of bear hides. Above the campfire stretched a long horizontal iron bar supported by two metal stakes driven into the ground on opposite sides of the stone fire pit. The bar held three hooks, each shaped like an elongated "S". One was empty. From another dangled a large blackened iron pot. The third hook was longer, holding a smaller pot suspended closer to the fire. Steam rose from simmering water. Andrew muttered something about having made the cooking equipment in much the same way as early European explorers to North America might have done.

A few minutes after Tom and Susan had returned to the beach, Andrew arrived. He nodded, and without saying a word he pushed the boat out into the bay, started the small motor and headed around the rocky outcropping. As he disappeared, the couple chuckled at the contradiction between Andrew's professed affinity for the 19th Century way of life and the gasoline motor propelling his aluminum boat. They were also concerned for his safety aboard the small fishing boat; the morning breeze had turned into a gusty wind.

They were starting to prepare lunch when Andrew steered his boat back into the bay and pulled up on shore.

"You folks heading back home soon?" Andrew asked. It was more of a statement than a question.

"In a little while," Susan answered. Tom was below deck doing maintenance on their boat. He stuck his head up as Andrew continued:

"Have you seen the sky?" Andrew added, suddenly talkative. "There's a big storm coming in from the south. You might want to head for a sheltered marina right way. You can keep your boat tied up here, but it won't be safe."

Andrew hurried up the trail to the ridge, presumably to prepare his camp for the coming storm.

Tom and Susan couldn't see much of the lake or sky from the narrow confines of the high rocky walls lining the narrow bay. A strip of shoreline was just visible directly east across the lake. They noticed waves on the lake had become larger than normal and the wind was continuing to pick up speed.

Tom and Susan climbed to the top of the rock outcropping. They looked south to the shore at the end of the lake five miles away. Usually, it was just visible on a calm day. Not now. Angry clouds and heavy rain obscured it. Waves appeared much higher in that direction than near their bay. Less than a mile away they spotted the infamous 'line' across the lake they'd been warned about. It foretold of a severe storm front. The storm was heading toward them, and fast.

The couple hurried back to the boat and quickly loaded their beach gear on board. They donned lifejackets, untied their big cruiser and headed for the mouth of the bay. As the boat emerged, it was hit by winds much stronger than the inexperienced sailors expected. The wind-whipped waves were at least four feet high. The boat swayed sharply. They secured and double-checked the canvas that enclosed the back and rear sides of the boat. The top of the canvas was attached with snaps to a fiberglass roof over the cockpit area.

Tom turned the boat into the growing waves as more experienced boaters had instructed him earlier.

High waves rose front and back. The wind screamed from behind. The flag on the bow snapped sharply forward. Waves splashed up on the rear canvas. Tom realized that strong waves could crash through the fragile canvas and swamp the boat. He had to keep the boat ahead of the waves that were chasing them from behind. He accelerated the boat. Within minutes the wind was blowing harder and harder. The waves kept increasing in size. They were now at a speed that maintained a precarious balance – just enough to stay ahead of the waves behind, but slow enough to keep from burrowing the bow too deeply into the waves ahead.

"Dear God, I sure hope the engine doesn't stall," Tom said. Susan nodded, looking scared for the first time in many years. She was not one to frighten easily. Loss of power would be a disaster. Left to the mercy of the waves the boat would be blown sideways. It would almost certainly capsize.

A large wave slapped up against the rear canvas. Water splashed into the boat between the canvas and the transom. Suddenly a few snaps holding the canvas came loose under the weight of another heavy wave. Then more snaps gave way. Gallons of water poured onboard. Susan rushed to the back ankle deep in water bucket in hand. Despite the pain of hands weakened by arthritis she managed to close the snaps. Meanwhile, Tom had accelerated the engines. The flag on the bow was limp. That was good. It meant they were keeping pace with the wind... and hopefully with the waves. But now the bow was digging deeper into the huge waves ahead. Avalanches of water broke over the bow again and again, engulfing the windshield, obscuring their vision. Tom and Susan estimated the waves were about six to eight feet high. They could barely make out landmarks on the shore through the driving rain.

Tom wondered how he was ever going to get the

boat through the tricky entrance into the marina in the raging storm. He drew small comfort from hope that if they crashed on the rocks trying to get in, people near the marina might see it happen and try to rescue them. Surely, he thought, someone will be there and have a rope to throw to them. He rehearsed in his mind how he would tie the rope first around Susan, and then hold onto the rope as best he could while they were pulled up over the rocks.

For the moment, Tom was maintaining a precarious balance between speed, wind and waves. The boat was making minimal headway, staying just ahead of the huge waves behind them. The waves in front kept crashing over the bow, flooding the windshield, blinding Tom and Susan. Every few minutes the boat plunged bow first into another breaking wave, again and again threatening to swamp the boat. But the plucky boat would emerge, after being almost totally submerged each time.

Finally, Susan saw through a side window a lakefront cottage they'd used as a landmark before. It was a mile south of their home marina. They were almost there!

The couple and their boat had been more than an hour battling the unforgiving lake. The trip from the beach normally took 20 minutes. Then they spotted through the heavy driving rain the rocky marina entrance. The couple looked at one another. In grim silence they agreed... yes, they would take a chance. They would try getting through the narrow entrance, despite the huge waves.

Tom tried to gauge carefully the rhythm of the waves, praying for a trough between them that he could use to power the boat into the entrance. He hoped that once past the outer rocks, the wave action would diminish, allowing him to navigate more easily the rest of the way through the entrance, and then into the calm water of the marina. It was a huge gamble. They went for it.

Tom got lucky—a bigger than normal trough between waves appeared with perfect timing. He hit the throttle, aiming for the center of the marina opening.

“Tom!” Susan screamed. “Watch out!”

Strong swirling winds caused by shore-based trees were overpowering the craft’s ability to navigate. The boat was slipping sideways toward enormous rocks on the port side, out of Tom’s line of sight. Susan scrambled to the port windows.

“Look out!” she cried. “We’re going to hit the rocks!”

Tom struggled to bring the boat about. It wasn’t working. The winds were too strong. He threw the engine into reverse, worried about wreaking the transmission. The boat shuddered then stopped. Tom accelerated the throttle. The boat slowly began to reverse against the howling wind.

Was it enough?

Tom gambled. He threw it back into forward again. The engine coughed. Tom’s heart sank. If the engine died they’d be doomed. Then it caught again. Tom thrust the throttle forward and spun the wheel to starboard. The boat crept ahead slowly. It was just enough.

They’d made it! In seconds, the wave action dropped to almost nothing.

Relieved, Tom made the final right turn into the marina. Both were startled to see people lining the sides of the large marina despite the wind and rainstorm. A few said later that 40 to 50 people were gathered. Tom and Susan wondered what they’d missed that had drawn such a big crowd. Then the crowd cheered and clapped. That’s when they realized... they were the attraction!

But Mother Nature was not through with them quite yet. Half way to their slip a rogue cross wind came barreling down a mountain valley next to the marina. The rogue gust caught the port side of the boat. There was no way to control it. In a second, the boat was forced sideways into the front of a large boat that for some reason had been docked backwards, improperly. The chrome hoop forming the 'pulpit' broke through their boat's starboard side windows just above the galley counter. After what they'd just survived, the couple looked at each other and burst out laughing.

From that day forward, other boaters in the marina considered Tom an experienced sailor. He was just happy they'd made it home safely. Later, Tom and Susan were told that the eight to 10 foot waves they'd encountered were just the early stages of the storm. Before it ended, gale force winds had created waves reaching 12 to 14 feet high.

It had been quite a weekend. They never forgot their chance encounter with the unusual stranger, Andrew, and his timely warning. It quite possibly saved their lives.

The Deer Finder

Wild deer came every day to drink at the narrow stream. Some had fawns, their tiny cinnamon-colored backs sprinkled with white dots. The stream bordered a clearing in the wilderness. A mineral salt lick rested on one bank; its purpose was practical and didn't include deer. But one majestic buck would soon die because of it.

That summer was unusually hot. Matt's parents worried their dozen milk cows and newborn calves might overgraze the small pasture on their farm.

"I need to talk to you," Matt's father said one day. He looked somber. Father and son were hauling hay into the barn. "Do you remember telling me about a clearning in the bush you found, last summer?"

"Sure," Matt said. "It's a couple of miles north of our fence line."

Matt remembered the clearing vividly. It was big, the size of a supermarket parking lot. The clearing was carpeted with tall succulent green grass, surrounded by dense underbrush and a forest of aspen and spruce. A small spring gave rise to a narrow stream that disappeared into the bush.

"I need you to take on a big responsibility now that you're on summer vacation," his dad said. "Do you think you could trail the cows up there every day after milking and bring them home in time for evening milking?"

"Sure!" Matt said eagerly.

He was 11 and grateful. This meant he'd escape the summer chores his mother always had for him and his two sisters. He didn't mind getting out of weeding the family's huge garden, cutting firewood, and painting fences and farm buildings.

Matt's new job began the next day. He and his dad, John, took their 12 cows and five calves up a narrow path to the remote grassy clearing. It was several miles away.

Matt herded the cows. John carried a heavy one-foot cube called a salt lick. The blue-tinted block contained minerals the animals needed to maintain good health.

Every day after that, Matt herded their cows up the narrow trail to the clearing after the morning milking and brought them home in time for the evening milking.

It was boring at first, watching cows chomp the grass... and defecate. *In and out . . . in and out*, he'd chuckled, trying to amuse himself. Even Towser, his aged border collie was restless for the first few days. The two found little for either of them to do. Heavy underbrush that surrounded the natural pasture discouraged exploration beyond its perimeter. The forest was almost impenetrable in most places, acting like a natural fence.

Towser and Matt habitually sat under a particularly large and bushy aspen tree on one side of the clearing. For the first few days, Matt watched Towser sniff and pee on just about every bush in sight. But finally he settled down and now was sleeping most of the day, evidently having decided that his ardent placing of territorial markings had done their job.

Then one day Matt began to *see* his surroundings as never before.

He began to take notice that all around... the air, the trees, the bush... were filled with creatures of all sorts, large and small, four legged, crawling and winged. And the deer came every day, often with single fawns or twins, unperturbed now by Matt and Towser's ongoing presence.

One day, Matt watched as a coyote wandered through the clearing. He was surprised when only a few curious cows raised their heads and then went back to grazing, unconcerned. A few days later, however, he again noticed a coyote. This time it was crouched behind bushes just beyond the clearing. The cows gathered in alarm, tucking their calves under their bellies. They bobbed their heads up and down, and side-to-side, snorting and bellowing toward the wild canine until it finally left.

Later, Matt learned that carnivores, such as coyotes and wolves, hunt not with malice or anger, but when hungry or needing to feed their young. Somehow, their prey knows the difference.

When he told his dad about the coyotes, John decided Matt needed more protection than Towser and his handmade walking stick. Although only 11, Matt had learned to use John's .22-caliber Winchester. It was a single shot rifle. Matt understood it could offer protection from an angry field mouse, but not much else.

Thus armed and guarded by a loving but aging dog that was terrified of gunfire and hid from thunder, the pair was set for the long daily vigils that lay ahead.

The sun was bright and warm on the day it occurred.

Towser was dozing again. Matt was struggling to stay alert, lest a hungry coyote or wolf on the prowl take an interest in one of the spring calves.

Squirrels were scampering around in the trees. They'd given up on scolding Matt and Towser. Birds of all types were chirping or squawking away, searching for insects and other tiny creatures to feed their young and themselves. Bees and horseflies and mosquitoes, and the dreaded black flies, droned above in search of nectar, or blood... human, canine or bovine... it mattered not.

With no warning, Matt's young mind became aware that he was immersed in the flow of Nature. He felt privileged to be experiencing it. Sadly, in just a few months, the joy of that experience would be repressed for years to come by another, more disturbing event.

In remote areas, farm families try to live on what they raise, or can hunt. Often, they pay no attention to hunting regulations; usually, no one bothers to enforce them. Wild game is needed to supplement their diets. That way, more farm-raised animals can be sent to market to earn scarce cash income.

Wilderness farmers hunt mostly in the late fall after harvest. They hunt in groups. It improves their chances. Proceeds are shared equally. In Matt's area they hunted for deer, elk and moose, and sometimes bear.

One evening, a group met at Matt's farm. Three farmers and his father, John, gathered at their kitchen table, along with Matt and one other farmer's son. The neighbor kid, Ben, was big; had to be 14 or 15, anyway, Matt figured. He was sure Ben knew a lot more about hunting than he did. In fact, Ben hinted he knew a bunch more about a lot of things. He was feeling superior and proud of it. Matt was intimidated, and annoyed at himself for falling prey to Ben's superior attitude.

The hunters began discussing places where they'd heard big game had been spotted in recent weeks. The locations were far away and would mean staying overnight. No one could afford RVs and there were no motels in the wilderness. It meant sleeping in tents possibly at below freezing temperatures, or in their pickups.

Matt could see the farmers weren't eager to face cold nights, and he wanted desperately to be included in the hunting party.

"I know a place where deer come to water," he volunteered. "It's not very far from here."

The conversations stopped, some in mid-sentence.

"North of our place," Matt added, turning to his dad. "You know... where I took the cows last summer. There's a little creek. The deer come there to use our salt lick and get water."

He'd pronounced it "crik". That was the grown-up way.

Matt had their attention. It made him proud. He could see that Ben was impressed and maybe a bit envious, too. That made him even prouder. He was one with them now. *Good for me*! he thought.

"Son, why don't you tell us about that clearning,"

John said. Matt understood his father wanted him to get all the credit. John already knew the location. Matt described for the others the route that Towser and he had taken with their cows each day during the two-month school summer vacation.

John asked Matt if he would show the hunters the way to the clearing. Matt's heart soared! He would get to guide all these grownups. Matt eagerly agreed. Now, he would *really* be one of them... a real hunter!

The men decided on a date for the hunt. It was a few days away. Earlier, John had made a point of showing Matt how to use his hunting rifle. The recoil from the .30-06 was fierce. Although John had shown him how to hold the rifle to minimize kickback, Matt still had ended up with a large bruise on his right shoulder. He was proud of it.

Matt showed off the bruise to his sisters, and displayed it proudly to his mother. She took note but Matt could see she wasn't all that excited about a big self-imposed blemish on her only son's skin.

Finally, the day of the hunt arrived. The hunters came to their farm early in the morning. Everyone was there by 3:30 a.m. The hunters would make their way north to the clearing in the dark. They wanted to set up a hunting blind and be ready well before first light.

Everyone was getting settled in the blind when John leaned over and whispered:

"Son, this is your find. It's only right that you get the first shot. Here, take my rifle."

Matt's pride leapt to new heights. His dad was going to trust him with his rifle! Until then, Matt thought his dad had trained him to use the rifle just to make him feel more like the other hunters. He liked the sound of the thought: *'just like the other hunters'*. Matt felt closer to his father that morning than he had ever been.

The other hunters were amused and indulgent as they watched the father and son. Perhaps they were remembering their own first hunts. Some had sons they'd trained, like Ben, who'd come along. *Boy*, thought Matt, *am I ever going show him a thing or two!*

Everyone settled down and waited.

Just as dawn began to show in the sky, John nudged Matt's arm, pointing cautiously through a slot in the piles of fresh-cut bushes in front of them forming the blind. There it was... a huge buck deer with a massive set of antlers.

The buck stood over the mineral block, eying it warily.

A pang of guilt came over Matt – he remembered that he was supposed to have retrieved the block, on his last trip home with the cows. By spring, it would be gone, disintegrated by the weather. Then he realized – hey, it may have been left behind but that's what had brought the deer to them. He was relieved; his father wouldn't scold him... not with a huge buck deer right in front of them, less than 30 yards away.

John nudged Matt again, smiling and nodding at his rifle. Matt was holding it in a safe manner as John had shown him. Matt had been so enthralled by the magnificent buck he'd forgotten all about the rifle.

Again, John nudged him and nodded once more, a bit impatient this time.

The buck lowered his head and sniffed the salt. He licked it. Suddenly he raised his head. He began sniffing the air and snorting quietly. Then he turned sideways to the hunters hiding in the blind.

Maybe he's heard or smelled us, Matt thought, worried.

The buck swung its head back and forth. He was acting more and more skittish. He moved his body slightly further away from the blind.

Matt felt everyone in the blind tense up.

Oh, oh! He thought. *He's going to run away.*

Matt lifted the weapon and steadied it on a stout branch. He peered down the barrel, being careful to center the sight just behind the deer's front shoulder, as he'd been taught. He pulled the trigger. The buck jumped and started to flee, then stumbled and fell. He was obviously dead. The bullet had pierced his heart.

A cheer when up from the other hunters. Matt's shoulder was hurting terribly. His dad hugged and congratulated him. Matt felt firm slaps on his back and shoulders. Even the older boy, Ben, thumped his back with his hand... a bit harder than he needed to, Matt thought.

"That was a nice clean shot," John told him. "You bagged a big one."

"Just like an experienced hunter," someone else added.

Matt accepted their compliments but didn't cheer. He wondered why at first. Then it came to him... he was feeling like a traitor.

From that day on he would feel guilt from having broken trust with what he had learned from Nature... with the privileged knowledge that had brought him and the other hunters to that special place. Above all, in his heart he knew he'd betrayed that magnificent buck deer.

Matt never went big game hunting again.

The Igloo

"Would you like to see a real igloo?" Bryan asked.

"You bet!" I replied.

And that's how easily I ended up caught in a deadly Arctic blizzard.

I was having coffee with a colleague at a restaurant in Inuvik, NWT, a village in Canada's high Arctic, when the ever-gregarious Bryan Redding joined us. He'd become famous by then. Many called him a 'white Inuit'.

Bryan invited us to visit one of his friends, an Inuit hunter, and the hunter's family. They were living in an igloo. The couple and their three children belonged to a nomadic community. It moved along the coast of the western Arctic following the wildlife that provided them with food, clothing and meager incomes. Bryan said the community was just a few miles away.

"I've always wanted to see an igloo up close," my colleague Eric said.

"Well, you'll see a whole community of them," Bryan said, chuckling. "It's about an hour north of here by snowmobile."

For Eric and I, making a quick trip to see a genuine igloo and to interview the family living in it, was irresistible. Turns out, not even Bryan expected that in the process he'd also be showing us how to build an emergency igloo at the height of a life-threatening blizzard.

We were in Inuvik on a news media junket. Our adventure that day was a side trip. We were among a group of journalists flown from Yellowknife, NWT, to the small community perched in the middle of the massive MacKenzie River Delta, to report on an announcement by some egocentric politician who wanted the dramatic setting.

With the noon-hour event over, Eric and I had adjourned to the town's only restaurant. The others were in the town's only bar. The plane flying us back south to

Yellowknife was scheduled to leave the next morning. With our news stories having been filed, Eric and I were killing time. That's when Bryan joined us.

"If we leave now, we could be back by suppertime," Bryan said.

"Well, let's do it then!" Eric replied.

Bryan was well qualified to be our guide. Few white men had the extraordinary skills needed to survive in the Arctic. Bryan did. He was 18 when hired by the fur-trading branch of The Hudson's Bay Company. For the next 15 years, he worked in several tiny communities scattered along Canada's 97,000 miles of Arctic coastline. He learned to live and hunt like the Inuit, and became fluent in numerous dialects of the Inuktitut (Inuit) language.

Bryan told us he'd hunted often with men from the community. We'd also heard rumors that he'd fathered children in a number of Inuit families. Wife sharing was a common practice at the time. The Inuit culture was quite different from our own.

Eric and I were city dwellers. We'd arrived in Yellowknife a week earlier to report on a session of the NWT's fledgling legislative government. We were ill equipped when the trip to Inuvik had come up at the last minute.

No worry, we both agreed. A quick side trip to see and photograph an igloo and back... what could go wrong? We assured each other we would be fine with our urban topcoats, gloves, wing-tip shoes and overshoes. Neither we, nor our employers, considered it necessary to invest in the knee-length hooded parkas, multi-layer wool and fir mittens, and sealskin mukluks everyone else was wearing. Big mistake!

We set off in the dark, even though it was early afternoon. In mid-winter there's very little daylight in the Arctic. What passes as daylight amounts to a few minutes of dawn just before noon followed by a few minutes of dusk, and then it's dark for the rest of the day.

I sat behind Bryan astride his snowmobile. Eric climbed onto another snowmobile behind Qamut, Bryan's Inuit friend. The machines roared northward. At times we were dodging low brush on the snow-covered tundra, other times almost flying across the frozen tributaries of the massive Mackenzie River Delta. It's the Arctic equivalent of the huge Mississippi River Delta some 3,100 miles south on the opposite coast of North America.

A half hour into our trip, I glanced back. There was no sign of our companions. I tapped Bryan on the shoulder with an already frozen hand. Lined leather gloves were no match for the 30 below F temperatures and wind chill from the speeding snowmobile.

Bryan pulled up.

He looked back, unconcerned.

"They'll be along," he said. "Give them a few minutes. Hop off if you like."

I did. Bryan laughed as he pulled me back up onto the snowmobile.

"Asshole!" I said, trying not to smile. "Damn your miserable hide!"

I'd sunk in the powdery snow up to my thighs. The light snow had gone up my pant legs and down into my overshoes.

Bryan said something in Inuit, still chuckling. I didn't understand.

"That's the Inuit word for this kind of snow," he explained. "The Inuit have 27 words for snow. Each word defines a particular kind or purpose."

Our companions joined us 15 minutes later. They explained that their snowmobile had stalled just a few minutes after setting out. Qamut had deftly stripped the engine down, cleaned out snow plugging an air intake and had the machine running again in short order. There are no auto clubs in the high Arctic.

My watch said it was late afternoon when we reached the Inuit community. The trip had been much longer than Bryan estimated. We arrived almost an hour past the time we intended to be heading back. I secretly prayed Bryan's navigation skills were superior to his grasp of the passage of time.

Through the gloom we could make out large white mounds on the otherwise almost flat snow-covered landscape. They were igloos, a dozen or so. Faint glows were visible from vent holes at the top of them, evidence of the seal oil lamps that supplied both light and heat.

"C'mon," Bryan cried as he leapt off his snowmobile. He dropped to his hands and knees on the hard-packed snow. Then he disappeared down a black hole. It was the entrance to a tunnel barely visible in the dark.

By now, Eric and I were so cold we could barely move. Our faces, eyebrows and hair were caked with snow and frost. We looked like actors in a winter scene from Leo Tolstoy's *War and Peace*. Our hands and feet had the dexterity of frozen boards.

We crawled toward the opening where Bryan had disappeared. I went first, dropping about three feet in a flurry of snow. Eric dropped behind me. We were in a short narrow tunnel. We crawled about six feet toward a faint light and then up a vertical incline, entering a wonderfully warm single room – the inside of the igloo. The temperature probably hovered just above freezing, but it felt almost tropical.

"Over here," Bryan said, now a dark shape lit slightly by two seal oil lamps. He introduced us to the man, a respected hunter, then to his kindly wife whose warm smile revealed several missing teeth, and then to their three small children.

The youngest child, a baby, was snuggled in the hood of the indoor parka the mother wore. The eldest child, five or six years old, was making shy while fussing with a toy made of whalebone. He or she – not obvious because of the parka – was sitting on a wide shelf about two feet above the hard packed snow floor. The shelf was four feet wide and surrounded the inside perimeter of the igloo. It was the family's living and sleeping area. The middle child, about two and naked from the waist down, was unmistakably a boy. Evidently he was not yet toilet trained. His excitement at seeing visitors initiated a yellow stream that arched away from him. It formed a pattern on the snow floor and promptly froze. The little boy was clad only in a shirt and tiny fur boots, but evidently was warm enough.

Later, I got a chance to whisper: "I checked, Eric. None of those kids looks anything like Bryan."

We both chuckled.

Our host motioned the four of us to sit on the shelf. It was covered in caribou and seal hides piled two to three inches thick. The family joined us. Eric and I were curious about how their igloo was built and their lifestyle. We began asking questions. None of the family spoke English and only Bryan spoke Inuit. With Bryan translating, and embellishing we suspected, the couple happily answered our questions in rich detail.

Suddenly a slab of something resembling a frozen steak appeared. Our hostess placed it on a flat piece of whalebone, produced a large knife and cut two-inch cubes from the foot-square slab. She gestured for us to help ourselves, then deftly lifted the fussing baby from her parka hood and began to nurse it, innocently oblivious to the strangers in her home.

Bryan and Qamut eagerly popped the frozen cubes into their mouths, as did the two older children. It was seal blubber, a staple food among Inuit across the Arctic. Eric and I exchanged glances and popped a cube into our mouths. We had to work hard at not gagging as our host kept passing us more cubes. Refusal would have insulted their gracious hospitality. Let's just say, frozen uncooked seal blubber has to be an acquired taste.

Before our hosts could insist on still more helpings of blubber, Eric and I whipped our cameras from the warmth next to our bodies and began taking pictures. The family happily posed for us. The light of the flashes ricocheted off the inner wall. I reached up and felt the glossy surface. Ice. Warmth from the igloo had melted the inner sides of the foot-thick building blocks and then froze, locking the blocks together and forming a solid barrier to drafts.

Brilliant, I thought.

"We'd better be on our way," Bryan said finally. He seemed uneasy about something. The brief visit was over.

I thought: *It's going to be a very late supper in Inuvik*, judging from how long it had taken us to get there. I hoped the hotel restaurant would still be open.

Moments later we were headed south toward Inuvik. That is, Eric and I assumed we were headed in that direction. A wild blizzard had roared to life while we were enjoying the hospitality of our hosts' snug igloo. Visibility was a few feet at best – we were in a whiteout.

"Awe, we're used to this," Bryan shouted encouragingly over his shoulder.

I sure hope so, I thought, holding my mouth closed to keep out the blowing snow.

The longer we travelled, the heavier the snow, the stronger the wind and the colder it got. Bryan finally stopped the snowmobile. I thought I'd never felt colder in all my life. Eric surely had to be feeling the same. He and Qamut were back there somewhere.

Bang!

One second I was sitting on the back of Bryan's snowmobile, the next I was draped backward over Qamut's windshield and the front of his machine. In the driving snow, Qamut hadn't seen us stop. He'd been concentrating on following the tracks of Brian's snowmobile and had run into the back of it at about 10 miles an hour.

"This is going to get worse," Bryan said, helping me up while shouting into my ear over the screaming Arctic wind. He ignored the accident after checking to ensure both machines were operational. "We'd better make camp." The worried look on his face was not comforting.

Bryan hopped back on his snowmobile and went searching for any form of shelter. There's not much in the high Arctic. He returned a few minutes later and led us to the leeward side of a low brush-covered hill. The unforgiving north wind was blowing clouds of snow over and around it, but at least it provided a bit of a windbreak.

Bryan got off his machine. The snow was hard packed under his mukluks. He pulled out a machete-like knife and plunged it into the snow. In seconds he'd cut loose a block of snow about 18 inches by 24 inches. He nodded at Qamut.

"We're going to build a snow house... an iglusuugyuk... to wait out the storm," he said. "Good snow here."

We learned an iglusuugyuk is an overnight snow house, a temporary version of an igloo built much the same way but smaller. They are used for temporary shelter. Blocks of snow for both are not rectangular, but resemble large bricks cut on an angle. Bryan and Qamut started with narrow wedge-shaped blocks of hard snow, placing them in a circle about 15 feet in diameter. The shape of the blocks created a spiral, around and around, leaning slightly toward the center and narrowing toward the top.

"You and Eric," Bryan shouted over the wind. "Get in the center. You can help us put the blocks in place."

We may have provided some legitimate help, but I'm convinced Bryan's primary motive was to give us some shelter from the howling blizzard. Soon we were ready to place the last blocks. Bryan stood on a larger square block he'd cut earlier and placed in the center. I wondered about the purpose. Now, I knew.

He reached up and placed the final blocks, leaving a small vent at the top. The large block he'd stood on later would become our table. Next, despite being in the dark, we helped dig the entrance, first tunneling down sharply, then out horizontally five or six feet, and then up to the outside. The result was a surprisingly effective air lock.

Trying to be helpful, I began cutting small blocks and placed them on the upwind side of the tunnel entrance, to act as a windbreak. Eric came to help. Bryan stopped us.

"The snow will drift over the top of your windbreak and down into the entrance," he shouted over the wind. "It'll plug it."

Sure enough, in just a few minutes drifting snow had begun to fill the entrance. We dug it out with our frozen hands. Eric and I removed the blocks and watched while the blowing snow passed right over the entrance. A little bit sifted down into the tunnel entrance, but not much. Lesson learned.

Back inside, Eric and I were surprised at how much warmer we felt out of the wind. Bryan and Qamut helped us smooth out the floor and then both went outside to move their snowmobiles into the shelter of the iglusuugyuk. They returned with arms full of goods from the storage hatches under the seats of their snowmobiles and a sled attached to Qamut's machine: sleeping bags, furs to sit on, a seal oil lamp with oil and wicks, matches, tin mugs and coffee, and of course a block of blubber. It tasted much better this time.

Qamut and Bryan chatted at length in Inuit while we ate and drank coffee heated over the seal oil lamp, luxuriating in the relative warmth. We could barely hear the wind through the foot-thick hard-packed blocks of insulating snow. But every so often, fine snow sifted down from cracks between the blocks above, reminding us of the raging gusts of wind outside swirling around our tiny shelter.

"We'll sleep in these," Bryan said, handing us sleeping bags. "The storm will blow itself out in a few hours."

"When's the next flight out of Inuvik for Yellowknife?" I asked. "Looks like we're going to miss tomorrow's flight."

"Friday," Bryan said.

This was Wednesday. Our editors wouldn't be happy about paying for extra hotel rooms and meals. Eric and I hoped our feature stories and photos about the family and their igloo would soften their disapproval.

I was in a deep sleep when Bryan shook my shoulder. He assured me it was the next morning.

"Time to go," he said, handing Eric and I each a few more cubes of frozen blubber. Frankly, I wasn't eager to leave the warmth of the Arctic-grade sleeping bag he'd loaned me, much less leave the iglusuugyuk. We discovered later, Bryan and Qamut had slept in their parkas, struggling to keep warm in sleeping bags not designed for an Arctic deep freeze. The two men normally covered their snowmobiles with those dirty and ragged old sleeping bags to keep the snow off.

We emerged to find the storm had blown itself out. But now, instead of swirling snow, all we could see in the darkness was a white expanse interrupted occasionally by snow banks or mounds, but otherwise absent of viable landmarks.

Somehow, Bryan and Qamut got us back to Inuvik, a testament to their consummate Arctic navigation skills. Turns out, the storm had grounded our flight overnight. It was scheduled to take off in a couple of hours.

Making Lemonade

Alan watched his four-year-old granddaughter Denise come skipping happily into the kitchen.

"What're ya doing, Grandpa?" she asked.

"Making my special lemonade for our company," he replied. "Your family will be here soon. Wanna help, sweetheart?"

"Yes!" Denise said. She pulled a kitchen chair over to the counter and scrambled up, eager for another fun experience during her sleepover.

"Your grandma invited your mom and dad and Erika to stay for Sunday dinner before taking you home," Alan said. "We're going to eat outside on the deck. It's very warm out there, so my world famous 'Grandpa Lemonade' is going to be mighty popular."

"Grandpa Lemonade?" Denise asked, a quizzical smile on her face. "What's that?"

"If you help, maybe I'll tell you the secret," Alan replied. "Okay?"

"Sure," Denise said happily.

"Okay then," said Alan. "I've cut all these lemons in half. Now, I'll squeeze each of them in this fruit squeezer. When that's done, can you put them in the recycling bucket for me? It will be a really big help!"

"Sure!" Denise said.

A few minutes later, Alan said, "There. All done. Now, I'm going to pour the juice into a big mixing bowl your grandma uses for chili. Then I'll add the rest of my very special ingredients, and presto we'll have my special lemonade."

"What special ingredients?" Denise asked.

"I usually don't tell anyone," he said. "That's 'cause only my 'rare and secret' ingredients can produce the wonderful mysterious flavor. Not even Grandma Patricia knows my recipe. But you're special, and I promised."

"Well, Grandpa," Denise said insistently. "What is it?"

"You've got to promise me that you won't tell anyone!" Alan said.

"I won't, Grandpa," she replied. "I promise."

"Okay, so here it is," he said. "To the lemon juice I add a little water, the juice of a few squeezed limes, some sliced lemons and sliced oranges for decoration, and a few ounces of pineapple juice for added sweetener. And that's it.

"You know, Sweetie," he added. "This is the very first time I've ever let anyone into the kitchen while making my famous lemonade."

Denise smiled proudly.

Alan began stirring the mixture with a big wooden spoon.

"Oh, there's the phone," he said. "Here, you hold the spoon while I go answer it, okay?"

In his absence, Denise decided to help her grandpa. Wooden spoon in hand, she began to stir Alan's famous brew. A big smile lit up her face. Now, she was really helping her grandpa!

"What in the world are you doing?" Alan exclaimed when he returned to the kitchen. He saw Denise leaning over the big stainless steel bowl, one hand planted firmly on the counter, the other thrust almost up to her tiny elbow in the lemonade, her arm swirling around. The big spoon was lying on the counter.

"You're not supposed to stir the lemonade like that!"

"I'm not stirring it, Grandpa!" Denise replied, near tears. "The spoon won't work! I can't get it with that!"

"Can't get what?" Alan asked, his eyebrows knitting together.

"My bubblegum!" she sobbed.

Perilous Waters

The wilderness farm where I grew up lacked many of today's creature comforts but we did have lots of water, even running water. Well, okay, my big sister and I did the running. We ran buckets of water into our farmhouse from a cast iron pump in the back yard.

In summer, the system was more sophisticated. Dad had rigged up a tank on a scaffold that collected rainwater from the roof of our house. He drilled a hole through the wall and installed a pipe to carry water from the tank to a tap above the kitchen sink.

It made our mother's life easier, and ours too. We used that water for most things. Mind you, we weren't allowed to drink the stuff. Occasionally, the tap coughed out bits of fur or feathers or decaying flesh we assumed came from some unfortunate critter that had exited the planet after falling into the tank. Our drinking water came from the hand pump. We used a stainless steel bucket to haul the water into the house where Mom protected it on the kitchen counter from flying critters and other contaminants with a freshly laundered dishtowel.

She needed water for almost everything: cooking, cleaning, washing clothes, and our Saturday-night baths. She heated water in a reservoir built into our huge cast iron wood stove, and in a kettle that simmered on top. Everyone took turns bathing in our galvanized tub on Saturday nights. The rest of the time the tub hung on a nail outside the back porch. After supper we'd drag it inside, into the middle of the cracked linoleum kitchen floor. Visitors from the city were dismayed to learn we all used the same water. Sometimes, the tub was pressed into use for emergencies. My sisters and I would learn all about that one embarrassing Sunday afternoon.

"Don't take too long," Mom would admonish us

before our turns in the tub. The reason was practical – the water got cold quickly.

Our little sister Bethany bathed first. As the second youngest, I was next, followed by my older sister, Carmen. While each of us bathed, Mom would enter the kitchen repeatedly with a dual mission in mind: to discourage play, and to add hot water from the kettle. We paddled our hands around vigorously to mix the welcome hot water with the cool. After our baths, we donned flannel pajamas and were sent upstairs to bed. Then it would be Mom's turn and, finally, Dad's. Our unlucky parents had to skim grimy crud off the murky water we'd left behind.

When the first frosts appeared in fall, it was time to drain the water tank. During the long cold months that followed, Carmen and I again supplied the running water, hauling it into the house and to roughs in the barnyard for our cows, horses, pigs and poultry.

During one particularly cold winter day we learned an important lesson: don't ever stick your tongue on a cast iron pump handle at 30 below zero.

"Oh et uhhy!" Bethany cried out. "I ut a ee."

Tears flowed down her chubby cheeks and onto the pump handle where they promptly froze, while she implored us to, "Go get Mommy", adding: "I have to pee." Darned if she didn't confirm the urgency of the latter. Wet marks appeared in a telling location on her snow pants, and promptly froze.

Turns out, it wasn't all that easy to liberate our little sister's tongue. Fortunately, Mom had the answer, as usual. It involved wrapping a succession of hot wet towels around the pump handle, keeping a safe distance on both sides from Bethany's firmly affixed tongue and the tender skin of her cherubic face. At first, the towels also froze to the pump handle. More hot towels were applied. Eventually, Bethany's tongue and the pump handle parted company.

Other water-based services on our farm differed considerably as well from today's accepted norms, including the disposal of wastewater. Our sewer service had two features: 1. my older sister's and my legs, and, 2. the family outhouse. The latter was positioned downwind a strategic distance beyond our back yard, tucked discretely behind Dad's garage. The disposal of wastewater also employed Carmen's and my young legs. Wastewater from the kitchen sink and debris from food preparation drained not down a sewer pipe, but into 'slop pails'. We carried out the slop, its odor enriched by potato, carrot and other peelings, table scraps and decaying leftovers. We dumped the mixture over a low bank into a deep depression on the far side of the back yard, not far from the outhouse. This low spot became a pond in spring. It would figure prominently in an adventure to come.

The other key component of our family's sewage system was that outhouse. The one-holer was a tall narrow structure clad with vertical boards of weathered wood. It stood guard at one end of a well-worn dirt pathway that formed a scar across a patch of ground-hugging weeds in the back yard we had the good humor to call a lawn. In winter, the path was often chest deep in snow.

An even less inviting chore was emptying the family's odiferous chamber pot, particularly in winter when it somehow tended to fill more quickly. Every few days one of us would carry out that precariously full white enamel container and dump its eye-stinging contents down the one-holer. We learned to pour with great care. One experience at cleaning our clothes and shoes from the consequences of faulty aim proved abundantly instructive.

Spring brought a welcome end to deep snow, fearsome blizzards and bone chilling temperatures. A spring creek drained snowmelt from a large pasture. It then flowed through the barnyard, and behind the garage and outhouse, before emptying into that low spot, turning it into a pond. And, yes, that's where we'd been dumping the bath water and slop pails all winter. Despite the toxic brew from various sources, the newly created pond proved irresistible.

"Let's build a raft!" I said one spring, the creative juices flowing. I'd just turned nine.

"Hey, great idea!" enthused Carmen, at 11 our self-appointed leader. "I know what we can use. There's an old pallet on the woodpile out back. Dad was going to chop it up for kindling." It became the centerpiece of our raft.

Before setting sail on the pond the first time, we had the foresight to remove our 'play' shoes and socks, and roll up our pant legs. Then we launched our raft and stepped on board. It promptly sank. There we were, up to our knees in a noxious mix our mother insisted would give us 'lock jaw', or some other calamitous affliction so unspeakably horrendous it defied even her awesome grasp of hyperbole.

The wannabe sailors persevered. We 'liberated' a tire inner tube from Dad's garage. It was the perfect solution to our flotation dilemma. Carmen and I took turns with a hand pump filling it with air. Bethany was six and deemed too little to pump. Then we hoisted our raft on top of the tube and launched the assembly into the pond. It worked well; too well, actually. Soon we were out in the middle of that body of brackish fluid, nicely dry but with no way of directing much less arresting our travel.

"I wanna go back!" Bethany cried, sensing our tension over being adrift. "I want Mommy!"

"Just hold on," Carmen counseled our little sister, invoking the superior wisdom of her senior age.

A breeze pushed us to shore. Off we went into the woods, returning with two freshly cut one-inch poles. Moments earlier, these innocent saplings had been minding their own business pursuing their destinies of growing up to become fence rails or lumber or firewood. Now, they formed part of our ship of dreams. All right, our raft.

Next, we budding sailors decided that our makeshift

craft needed an anchor. We knew nothing about such things. Besides, we had no rope. I wondered if some other device might do the job. We tried the poles. No luck. Even when sharpened at one end as best we knew we couldn't sink them deeply enough into the squishy bottom to secure our raft. Back we went to Dad's garage. By this time our little sister had become far too intrigued to even consider retreating to our mother's skirts, thereby 'blowing' our covert adventure.

"Hey, look at this!" I said. "I bet it'll work great!"

A four-foot metal rod was leaning against the wall. Once upon a time, the rod had served as the transmission shift lever for a big truck. A round plastic knob was affixed to one end. The other end came to a sharp point. Dad used it to chip ice from the livestock watering troughs in winter. It was spring. He wouldn't need it any time soon.

One Sunday morning, we were told company would arrive that afternoon. It proved a fateful day for us mariners.

After lunch, Mom sent us upstairs to don our finest clothes. Now, in our farm neighborhood only two occasions warranted dressing up on Sunday: church and company. She sent us outside to play, adding her favorite double-barreled admonition: "go outside and have fun, but don't get dirty". She never confessed to the contradiction.

Dejected, my sisters and I parked our well-clad bums on freshly swept wooden steps leading down to the back yard from the porch. We were impatient and bored awaiting the company, close friends of our parents. They were childless. With no kids, they weren't *our* company. As we sat on the porch steps whining to each other about our lost playtime, I had a thought:

"While we're waiting, let's go sailing on the pond!"

As if on cue, the three of us glanced around furtively, fearing discovery. After all, Mom insisted she had eyes in the back of her head, and often seemed able to prove it. Luckily, she was off fussing over something vitally important in the house. Dad was busy in the barn doing things equally significant. Clumps of willows and trees partly obscured the pond from the house and barn. It was a no brainer.

We were vaguely aware that water in the pond originated from the large cow pasture beyond our barn. The snowmelt stream flowed through the barnyard, then behind our outhouse and into the pond, carrying a rich mixture of soil, cow manure and who knows what else. And of course that brackish mixture was further enriched by a winter's accumulation of frozen bath water and kitchen slops, now thawed and melding with the water-borne sediments arriving from the pasture and barnyard. A charming stew!

The lure of sailing on that pond was unrelenting. We reasoned that once the company had gone our parents would be less distracted and more alert to our misadventures on the pond, and would thus be more likely to apprehend us. Besides, by then it would be time for our afternoon chores, and that would preclude for sure a sail that day.

We gave in to temptation. The final incentive was the confidence we had in our tube-supported raft. So, despite being dressed in the best clothes our family's strained budget could afford, we made our way surreptitiously to the pond and set sail. Soon, the three of us were happily poling our way around in the middle of that iniquitous liquid.

"Hey guys," Carmen said. "Let's anchor a while. We've got time."

"I'll get the anchor," I said, proudly grabbing the sharpened steel rod we'd taken along. My plan was to ram the sharp end between the wood slats of the raft and into the bottom of the pond, anchoring our raft in position. We'd done it before. I proceeded to do so.

We're not sure what happened next. Perhaps it was

a wave or someone moved. But you guessed it: my aim was off, just enough. The steel rod went through the upper side of the tube, then through the bottom, creating two large air leaks. I realized what I'd done, and instinctively pulled the big steel rod out of the tube. Wrong! With the rod pulled, the air escaped even more quickly.

"We've got to get to shore fast!" I shouted.

"Oh damn!" Carmen said, bringing to bear the strongest curse word in her repertoire at the time.

"I want my Mommy," said Bethany, invoking her most urgent petition for salvation.

We poled hard for shore. Not good enough! The water rose quickly over our 'dress' shoes and then our ankles. Suddenly, it was up past the knees of our best clothes. We jumped overboard trying to get to shore more quickly. We misjudged the depth. The murky water came up to my waist, and to our little sister's chest.

With abundant cause for acute trepidation we took our soggy selves to the back door where we were greeted by a deafening shriek:

"What in the world? What have you done?" The pitch of Mom's voice rose with each word. Her question was rhetorical; she knew exactly what we'd been doing.

We shouldn't have been surprised when ordered to stand in line on what passed for our lawn. We were directed to scrub each other's clothing with a coarse brush, as she poured bucket after bucket of cold water over us, pumped vigorously by Dad.

"Now, get those clothes off!" Mom growled, her anger unabated. Dad dragged the bathtub into the kitchen, despite the imminent arrival of the company. Then he hauled cold water straight from the pump until there was six inches of it in the tub while we stood around outside shivering in our once-white, now grimy underwear.

"Listen to me!" Mom shouted, her voice once again countless octaves above our comfort zone. "Each of you will get into that tub and scrub yourselves down with lots of soap! Do... you... hear... me?"

We nodded sheepishly.

Bethany was first. I was next. The viscosity of the cold water in the tub had evolved well beyond grimy long before it was Carmen's turn.

The company knocked on the back door. This was the usual point of arrival at farm homes. But it meant they would walk through the kitchen, behind Carmen and the tub, to reach our seldom-used living room, kept meticulously groomed for such occasions. They chuckled as they strolled by. Poor Carmen! She was obliged to crouch in the tub seeking desperately to protect her pre-pubescent modesty.

It didn't take my parents long to identify the main culprit in our failed nautical adventure. My sisters willingly concurred, the monsters! They were right, of course. After all, going sailing had been my idea, and it was I who'd poked the holes in the tube.

"You're going to empty the tub," Dad said. It would be the atonement for my culpability. But I noticed again, as I had before, that his stern demeanor failed to conceal a glimmer in his eyes. In later years, I would learn that glimmer had more to do with recollections of his childhood misbehavior than with current events.

Dad insisted I dump the buckets into our infamous pond. I could have used the nearby garden. Besides, the water carried a fertilizing element. The pond was 200 feet farther. The truth was, that more distant trek was part of Dad's notion of my richly deserved punishment. The first few buckets went fine. But with each trip, they felt heavier and the contents became more brackish. At long last, I was scooping the remnants from the tub. It was mostly watery brown mud, bearing a striking resemblance to liquid manure.

Just then, I heard Mom come into the kitchen to

make tea for their company.

"What in the world?" she cried as she walked behind me.

Suddenly, the ladle I'd been using was snatched from my hand. It bounced with a gentle whack on the top of my head. Turns out, she objected to me using that ladle to empty the tub. Perhaps it's because the thing came from our bucket of drinking water on the counter. Hey, I would have rinsed it out before putting it back. Honest! Well, okay, I'm pretty sure I would have.

Terry's Story

A Modern Day Old-Fashioned Love Story

Terry was a pretty high school student with a bubbly personality, honor grades, and a circle of close friends.

"Life was good," she said. "Best of all, John and I were dating."

They'd started going out when John was 16. She was 15. Within a year, they became 'an item' among the high school crowd in their small town.

"I liked John a lot," Terry said wistfully. But she also admits that at the time she was feeling conflicted.

Terry was attending a Roman Catholic school. Like many other students, she was counseled toward considering a religious vocation. She'd developed a need to explore that as a career. For her, it would mean becoming a nun. But Terry also knew that she was drawn to a far more appealing option: John.

She had to be sure. So, Terry entered a convent during her final year in high school. She was 17. A year later, she returned home, convinced a religious life was not for her. John was still waiting. She knew then that only John could make her life complete.

Soon after, he asked her to marry him. Terry was ecstatic.

Usually, that's how fairytales go. Right? Not this time.

It was the 1960s. Religion had a powerful influence over many families. Terry's parents belonged to one religion; John's parents believed in another. That didn't concern Terry and John, at first. They paid no attention to such things. After all, they had each other. That would be enough, or so they thought.

John's parents supported Terry and John's plans to marry. What the couple hadn't counted on was fierce opposition from Terry's father. Despite her tearful pleas, he was adamant. He refused to reconsider. Ultimately, it broke their hearts. Terry and John were forced to go their separate ways.

Eventually, Terry and John married others. In the years that followed, each raised families, pursued careers, and experienced the triumphs and tragedies of life. Their separate well-ordered lives cruised along for decades. And then tragedy struck. Both lost their spouses just a few years apart.

"I loved my husband," Terry said. "We had a wonderful relationship. I was blessed. But during all that time, never a day went by that I didn't think about John, wanting him to be happy and well. There were no thoughts of disloyalty. I'm not made that way. I even told my husband about John... he said it proved to him that I knew how to love. It was a gift, he said.

"Wasn't I lucky to have someone like him? I have to admit, just remembering the feelings that John and I shared all those years ago, would often warm my heart. I think it made me a more caring person."

John freely admits also that Terry was on his mind persistently throughout those 50 years.

"I would hear her wonderful laugh in my mind, and often feel buoyed by the joyful sense of humor I'd experienced with her," John said.

On rare occasions, John and Terry's growing families would encounter each other in parks and restaurants in their hometown. Terry still lived there; John and his family lived in a town a few miles away. Both Terry and John admitted there would be an emotional twinge, at first, but it passed. The four parents and their children would mingle happily, leaving the past firmly in the past.

Terry's career led her to study accounting, ultimately becoming a supervisor in an accounting firm.

John's route in life was more unusual.

Fifty years ago, a high school graduate could become a teacher with just a few months of training. So, at 19, John not only became a teacher in the elementary school of a small rural town, but he also became the principal.

He was nicely settled into his career and raising his family when he and his wife agreed to take over a pizza restaurant and an ice cream shop owned by his wife's retiring parents. Both businesses were located in a summer resort, not far from John's school.

During the school year, he would be focused on school. But when summer came, John and his wife were kept busy running the pizza restaurant and the ice cream shop.

Then, tragedy struck. John's wife died unexpectedly of a heart attack. In his grief, he found solace by focusing on his family, his career in education, and his business interests.

A few years later, tragedy struck Terry's life. Her husband died of cancer. She found comfort in her family and career. In time, Terry began to get on with her life. She didn't want to be alone. She had a few relationships.

"Those came and went," Terry said with a wry grin. "I have no regrets. You could say those experiences left me a bit wiser."

One day, quite by accident, Terry and John met. They went for coffee. The pair hadn't had contact for several years. The former teenage sweethearts got caught up on their recent histories. They decided to meet again for a coffee, and then again. They began seeing each other.

At first, they were uncertain, tentative even, about their rekindled attraction for each other. Those feelings had been tucked away 'safely' for many decades. Neither dared to call it 'dating'. They told family and friends: "We see each other occasionally". But that wasn't exactly true.

Terry knew. So did John.

"My heart soared every time I saw John, or heard his voice on the phone," Terry said, a huge smile lighting up her radiant face.

Those occasions became more and more frequent. Still, their unease persisted. After all, half a century had passed since they'd been high school sweethearts.

One day, John told Terry that he was going to the Florida Keys for a few weeks. It would be a combined business and recreation trip. Terry's heart fell. Now that she'd found John again, the thought of being apart from him for that long was more than she felt she could bear.

Then to her surprise and delight, John invited her to accompany him. He explained that he had a condo on one of the keys (islands). He quickly reassured her the condo was a two-bedroom unit. She would have her own room and her own private bath.

The separate accommodation lasted for most of the first night.

The lovers were reunited – a modern day Romeo and Juliet story... but this time, with a much happier ending. A year later they were married, coming full circle on a journey 50 years after it all began.

Comin' Down The Mountain

Bad decisions can make good stories. Here's one.

It was mid-summer and we'd set off to find bike trails at our local ski resort. Cycling on ski runs? The concept had become popular. Regardless, the contradiction was intriguing.

Silver Star Ski Resort had begun to operate year round. In winter, it offers traditional downhill and cross-country skiing. And now in summer, like others, it had opened many of the ski runs for cycling. We wanted to explore this. Turns out, most of those runs were for extreme motocross cyclists. We didn't know.

Sharolie and I drove up to the forested ski hill imagining trails suitable for seniors. You know, the gently descending and mostly horizontal kind. Counterintuitive on a ski hill, perhaps, but still we were assured that such trails did exist.

When we arrived, the resort village was bustling with athletic young bodies, most of them half our age. All right, a third our age. Okay, okay . . . a few were almost a quarter our age.

They were all padded up: helmet with facemask, knee and elbow pads, shin and forearm pads, thigh and upper arm pads, ankle pads and padded shoes, not to overlook chest and belly pads, back pads, toe pads and crotch pads.

Whew! While it wasn't clear which trails they were heading out on, this nubile assemblage looked much like a curtain call for an episode from Star Wars. Whatever they were up to, their outfits and their bikes looked mighty serious. We learned their 'rides' ranged in price from around $3,000 for an economy model, up to the equivalent of the down payment on a reasonably good used car.

We self-consciously checked our outdated helmets and pretended to busy ourselves limbering up the old fashioned brakes on our 'rides', undeterred by those casting furtive glances at our 30-year-old solid-frame mountain bikes. So what if ours were much older than most of those youngsters directing bemused looks our way?

"Well, hell," I said to Sharolie. "We came here to find those trails on the cross-country ski runs you talked about, so let's do it!"

We bought day passes. The guy behind the counter gave us directions to the first of the 'easy' trails we'd spotted on the map. He confirmed those were fairly level trails i.e., good 'starter' trails.

The guy (I swear, he'd just graduated elementary school) pointed on the map to a colored route close by. Sharolie confirmed it looked just like one of the cross-country ski runs she'd been on last winter. Seemed like a good place to start.

"Go out here and turn left," the kid said. "Then take a right. Look for Easy Street. It'll take you there."

Easy Street?

We liked the sound of that.

I'm just sayin': if anyone shows you a map of Silver Star Mountain and points to a trail called "East Street", don't believe it!

We set off in search of "Easy Street". After looking around for 15-20 minutes we stumbled upon a sign that said, "Easy Street". Ah, finally! The fact is we should have gone no further. We went on. Turned out to be one of those bad decisions.

Off we went along a well-worn trail covered in an inch of powdery ochre-colored dirt. It was fairly level at first. Then the trail turned down and to the left – that is, it banked sharply and dropped steeply, as in, a 45-degree angle, maybe more.

After easing my way around a couple more hairpin turns and down precipitous drops, I found a place to pull over. I began walking my bike down the steep trail and around the sharp hairpin turns. I'd lost sight of Sharolie. I started back, worried about her. Not smart.

Every so often, one or two capeless Darth Vadar look-alikes whizzed by, alarmingly close, their two-wheeled cannon balls barely touching the ground.

"What to you think, Love?" Sharolie asked when she caught up. "Should we turn back?"

Now, I wouldn't describe that look in her beautiful hazel eyes as fear. She's fearless. But for sure, it was a look of serious concern.

Being unwilling to give up easily (okay, stubborn), I made a decision. It wasn't the right one, again.

"Maybe this is a link down to our trail," I ventured. "You know, maybe this trail we're on is one of those that funnels everyone away from the village and onto the various trails."

Sharolie didn't seem convinced. Frankly, I wasn't either.

Another squadron of wannabe Darth Vaders went whooshing by.

Praying that the Star Wars curtain calls were over, we carried on. Immediately, we wished we hadn't. The very next bend was a nasty hairpin leading to a particularly sharp drop... one of those no-return experiences you sometimes find yourself unwillingly committed to while emitting a heart-felt, "Oh Shit!"

The purpose for hairpin turns was obvious. They're banked steeply to prevent riders from going off the trail into the trees. Now, guarding this next sharp bend was a grove of stout aspen trees, their trunks six to eight inches in diameter. Going off trail at a high speed and hitting them... well, it could spoil your whole day.

"Hey, look down there," I said to Sharolie, pointing. "A level trail!"

What a novel concept!

Through the trees about 100 feet below we saw riders streaming along a level trail. We didn't know where it went or where it had come from, but didn't care. We set out to find it.

Down more steep inclines and around more precariously tight hairpin turns and suddenly we were on the level trail. We followed it down a few more mercifully gentle slopes and even gentler turns. Suddenly we came upon an opening in the evergreen forest.

A heavy metal railing appeared on our right. Good thing. Beyond was a 50-foot drop. The rusted railing funneled us toward a large structure. Here, those Darth Vadar lookalikes were handing their bikes to attendants, who were attaching them to moving metal brackets. Then, they hopped into seats and were whisked upward.

"Hey, it's the six-man chair lift!" Sharolie exclaimed while I was trying to make sense of things.

Both of us were coated in ochre-colored dust, but relieved to be on our own two feet. We made our way to people who looked to be employees. We began explaining how we got there. All but one of them drifted away – probably to share a private 'guff-haw' with others. No matter.

"How do we get back to the village?" I asked our contact. He'd introduced himself as Rudy. He seemed to be in charge.

"That's it," he said, pointing to the chair lift. "You need a pass."

"It goes all the way to the summit," Sharolie said helpfully. That would be 6,300 feet.

"If we took the chair lift, how do we get back down to the village?" I asked again. It seemed like a logical question worth repeating.

"The ski trails," Rudy answered matter-of-factly.

We were standing near the metal rail. I looked over. Far below, dump trucks were going back and forth on a gravel road. *Why not a couple of bikes, too?* I thought.

"What about that road?" I said.

"Afraid not," Rudy said. "Bikes aren't allowed on the road. Too dangerous."

Tell me about danger, I thought.

I began plotting how we might sneak away from the ski lift into the bush and find our way down to the road. Screw permission; I'd worry about forgiveness later. Sharolie wasn't keen on the road option. Reluctantly, I agreed. That was a good decision.

I could see Sharolie was excited about the prospect of using the chair lift.

"How do we get on?" she asked.

"A pass," Rudy repeated.

"We don't have passes for the chairlift," I said. "We got day passes to use the *easy* trails," I said, emphasizing 'easy'. "Someone sent us down here."

Judging from the map, it was probably a 500-foot climb back up to the village. Evidently, the only option was to climb our way back upstream on the trail against the steady down of pseudo Star Wars traffic. Oh yes, that would be while lugging our bikes.

Ugly prospect.

"Can we buy passes here?" Sharolie and I asked as one.

"No," Rudy replied. "You need to have your passes when you get here."

Then, his eyes flashed one of those, 'Oh what the hell!' looks.

Rudy shrugged his shoulders. "Forget the passes," he said, sending a hand signal to a couple of young employees. "Do you know how to get on?"

"No," I said, truthfully.

"Yes," Sharolie said, truthfully. She skis, I don't.

We watched as the attendants took the bikes from others in line ahead of us and loaded them. The owners jumped into the seats that swept around next. Then, it was our turn. Almost immediately, we were a few hundred feet above the mountainside.

Within minutes we were at the summit of 6,300-foot Silver Star Mountain, astride our reasonably serviceable but admittedly aging mountain bikes. I glanced quickly over my shoulder in time to see the chair lift disappear down over the side of the mountain. I felt this odd sensation of abandonment. You know, like those nightmares you had as a child of being abandoned by your parents on a street corner?

Now, the only route to safety really was biking all the way down the side of the mountain. Mixed feelings about that; it would be a long walk if one of our bikes failed.

Ahead of us was a huge billboard showing the various ski runs in winter and those converted to bike trails in summer. Most looked much too vertical.

"There," said Sharolie. "That's the one I told you about. The Paradise run."

We got closer. I was a tad skeptical after falling prey to 'Easy Street'. We scoured the map. Yup, the Paradise run seemed the lesser of the evils. It promised to bring us to the ski village in just five miles.

The first couple of gentle switchbacks brought a feeling of relief to both of us. Half way to the next turn the trail turned soggy. We looked into the bush on the mountainside to our right – huge banks of snow. Hey, this was mid-July. The forecast high for the day in town was 95 F (35 C). It seems that snow can be tenacious at this altitude.

Then it started.

Swoosh! Thump! Swoosh! Thump!

"What's that?" Sharolie asked.

We looked up into the trees above our trail.

There they were again. The Darth Vadar wannabes in action!

Turns out their extreme trails would intersect our gentle trail many times en route to the village – theirs mostly vertical, ours mostly horizontal.

We had to listen very carefully... especially for the occasional single motocrossers. Those were the dangerous ones – hard to hear them coming.

Mostly, they came in tight squadrons of threes and fours:

Swoosh! Thump!

Swoosh! Thump!

... the sounds of them swishing down the almost vertical trails that intersected our trail, and then landing jumps above us... or below us... or both.

And then they were gone.

Or were they?

Swoosh! Thump!

Swoosh! Thump!

Not quite. Mercifully, the village soon came into view through the forest.

Would we do it again? You bet! The same way? Not a chance. We'll pay the $20 lift charge. Hey, it gets you three trips up the mountain.

Grandfathers Are Antique Boys

He acted like a little boy at times. That's how he got four grandsons into trouble one day. It all started over lunch.

Grandpa's daughter (their aunt) was getting married the next day. The family had gathered from far and wide. Grandpa offered to take the four pre-teen boys out for a few hours. It would give the stressed parents a break.

The plan was for them to make two stops. The first was at a store to spend money he'd sent them at Christmas. Then, he'd take them for lunch. The spend-and-eat thing was Grandpa's favorite outing with his grandchildren.

The shopping was hilarious. It took a while for the boys to get focused – the 'kid in a candy store' thing. Finally, each managed to squeeze his dreams into his budget, more or less, thanks in part to Grandpa's 'topping up'. Soon, every grandson had a suitable treasure clutched in his hands. Then it was lunchtime.

Off they went to a nearby restaurant. The place was crowded. It took 15 minutes to get seated, and longer to get menus. The boys were ready to order seconds after the menus arrived. What's complicated about macaroni and cheese, or grilled cheese sandwiches? But the server had left. Placing the orders became an endurance test. The five huddled in the booth, watching as servers rushed around delivering food to just about everyone else.

Well now, Grandpa enjoys the company of his grandchildren. He loves them all – the babies, the toddlers and especially those in their pre-teens. He admits he enjoys most of all mixing it up with the older boys. They have wrestled and tickled, and hugged, and he has played games outside with each of them. That gave Grandpa an idea.

Jon was sitting directly across from Grandpa. A cousin sat on each side of him. Another cousin, Will sat beside Grandpa. Jon placed his hands on the table, one on top of the other. Grandpa put his right hand on top of them. Jon withdrew his bottom hand and placed it on top of Grandpa's. Then Grandpa put his left hand on top of Jon's. The others joined the hand-stacking game. The pile of hands increased in height and then in speed... faster... and faster... and faster. Their hands finally disassembled and they dissolved in peals of laughter.

But they weren't finished with the games quite yet. Hey, they were still waiting for service. Grandpa grabbed Jon's right hand. It was familiar – their arm-wrestling mode. They'd done it many times. Their clenched hands wavered back and forth. Grandpa always faked it. He let Jon push his grandfather's hand down almost to the table... but not quite. He pushed Jon's hand up and then down the other way until Jon's hand was almost at the tabletop. Then he let it come back up to the middle. The other boys understandably were cheering their cousin. They were certain Jon could 'take' Grandpa. He was old, you know!

In a booth across from them, a 20s-something couple was enjoying the contest. The man urged on Jon. The woman wore a faint smile on her attractive face. But not everyone was enjoying the impromptu entertainment. Two elderly women in the booth next to the young couple kept frowning and clucking their mutual disapproval to one another over the spectacle across the aisle.

Back at the arm-wrestling contest, the grandsons were not to be denied. Jon recruited allies. First, cousin Joey added his right hand to the clasped hands of Jon and Grandpa. All the boys began to cheer. Grandpa had no trouble managing two opponents. The other two boys noticed. So, Casey joined the boys' team. More cheering. Still Grandpa prevailed, but he was just barely holding his own by now.

Will was sitting next to Grandpa. He was the youngest, but big for his age. He got set to join his cousins. Grandpa called him a traitor to their side of the booth. Ignoring the criticism, Will added his hand and considerable weight to the pile of hands. Grandpa's arm began to waver, but he was holding on. Then Will stood up and put one knee on the seat, bringing the force of his weight to bear. Grandpa's arm wavered and then came crashing down.

The boys cheered loudly. In several parts of the restaurant, people were standing to see what was going on. The couple across the aisle joined in the merriment – the young man cheering, the woman smiling indulgently. The old ladies, frowning, tut-tuted even more and readied their purses for a hasty escape from this unruly behavior.

And then, as if by some miracle, a flustered server arrived in a rush and took the orders. By another miracle, the meals arrived in record time... in just a few minutes... just as the boys and their grandfather were getting started on another contest. Imagine that!

When Grandpa went to pay the bill, the cashier smiled at him and chuckled self-consciously. She knew what he knew—that he knew exactly how to speed up service.

How to Shrink-Wrap A Cottage

Our friend Ken Hagerman was an unrepentant practical joker. When he and Donna left a friend's home after a visit, the hosts were sure to find pictures turned upside down, their bed short-sheeted, or pebbles in the toes of their shoes – or all three. But to his credit, Ken also was one of those special folks who enjoyed practical jokes played on him. It wasn't quite as much fun, he would admit, but when someone 'got him' he was the first to congratulate the perpetrator. And of course, he immediately began to plot revenge.

Ken and Donna were friends and neighbors in town. We were delighted when they also became neighbors at the lake. During the summers that followed, both couples often would be at the lake at the same time. Then, practical jokes between Ken and I could become frequent events, much to the chagrin of our spouses and the delight of our neighbors.

One summer, we were on vacation at the lake when Ken and Donna called one Monday morning to say they would arrive Friday afternoon. But a few days later, Ken phoned again to say they'd be delayed until Saturday night.

What a golden opportunity for a practical joke on Ken! Neighbors jumped at the chance to get even for jokes he'd played on them. We hatched a diabolical plot. It would catch Ken totally unaware. We took delight knowing this one was going to put us one-up on the King of Practical Jokers.

Here's how the plot unfolded.

When Ken and Donna bought the property the previous owner had left behind a huge roll of clear film wrap. It had remained untouched under the picnic table on the covered deck. For the conspirators, the plot was a no-brainer. We would 'shrink wrap' Ken and Donna's cottage.

We guessed it would be dark when Ken and Donna were due to arrive Saturday evening. They wouldn't notice until the last minute. With the shrink-wrap firmly in place, they'd be unable to open the door or figure out the problem easily in the dark.

It was perfect... made in Practical Joke Heaven.

So, three neighbor men took turns helping me unfurl the heavy roll of 24-inch wide shrink-wrap. The roll weighted close to 50 pounds so it took two to manage the thing. First, two unfurled it down the front of the 35-foot cottage, being careful to cover the door. Then the other two conspirators took over, unrolling the shrink-wrap down the far side of the cottage and across the back, keeping it tight. The pairs took turns. Around we went, four times, five times, and then six times, maybe more, sealing the door tightly.

Saturday morning arrived. The conspirators were smug, and beside themselves with delight over the practical joke they'd played on 'The King'. But waiting to catch Ken in the act of trying to open the door to their place was going to be difficult.

Saturday was blistering hot, as it had been on Friday when the deed was done.

Evening came, offering scant reprieve from the oppressive heat. No sign of Ken and Donna. The conspirators and their spouses began to worry. Eventually, everyone retired for the night. All night there was no reprieve from the oppressive, sticky heat.

Sunday came and with it another blistering hot day. Still there was no sign of Ken and Donna. It was, after all, a long weekend. So, our friends still had Monday. Monday morning, promising to be as hot as the previous days, the errant couple arrived. We could see from our hiding places that they were sweaty, tired and delighted to finally be at the lake. As they emerged from their vehicle, we heard them spoke to each other eagerly about getting into shorts and out on the lake in their boat.

We waited impatiently, out of sight, listening for audible signs that our practical joke had hit a bull's eye. Nothing. Half an hour later, still nothing.

The suspense eventually became too much for my fellow conspirators and me. We decided to sneak up to Ken and Donna's place. We were not proud at all of what we came upon.

Ken and Donna were there, and they were busy. Ken was packing filled garbage bags into the back of his truck. He was not in a pleasant frame of mind. Donna was handing Ken another full garbage bag. She was even unhappier than Ken.

Eventually, the truth emerged. Our practical joke had backfired... and in a very unpleasant way.

With amazing restraint, Ken and Donna informed us the shrink-wrapping had blocked the vent on their fridge at back of the cottage. Heat had built up, tripping the circuit breaker. Both the fridge and the freezer had shut down. Several dozen pounds of frozen meat had turned rancid and smelly in the unseasonably hot mid-summer weather. An assortment of other foods also spoiled.

Oops!

We slinked away, deeply embarrassed and humbled, as we should. Our spouses said so too, just to make sure.

Us four bandits offered to replace the lost food, but to no avail. Ken and Donna made it clear, graciously somehow, that they would have none of it. Then the four of us decided each would secretly leave peace offerings. During the next few days, the offerings appeared on Ken and Donna's deck, in the form of their favorite wines, beer and rum.

But just as mysteriously as the peace offerings appeared, over the next few days they somehow showed up back on the exact deck of the very conspirator who'd made that particular offering. That is, the beer made its way back to the beer donor's deck. Ditto, for the bottles of red wine and white wine, and the rum.

Nothing more was said by anyone about the day we shrink-wrapped Ken and Donna's cottage. Make no mistake. Ken got the last laugh, not surprising. Those never-uttered last words spoke loudly.

The practical jokes carried on until the day Ken died unexpectedly a few years later of a heart attack. A few weeks earlier, my wife and I had been graced by a visit from him and Donna. A few hours after they left, we found that a picture was turned upside down in our back porch. It still is.

Finding Plato

People of a 'mature persuasion' know these things to be true: When having problems with your computer, ask your kids for help. If it's urgent, ask your grandchildren.

And so it came to pass one day in our den. Our family had just received our first computer with all of the usual accouterments: monitor, keyboard, tower, printer, router, modem... you know the drill. The fellow from the shop hooked up everything in a flash. He gave us a primer course on how to operate everything. It took even less time than the installation. No matter—my wife and I didn't understand a thing he said.

Now, much of my career was spent working for high-tech companies. I made a determined effort to keep up with the latest developments in digital technology, fiber optics and the Internet. The truth be known, that effort did more to generate a false sense of aptitude than it did to instill any semblance of practical knowledge.

Fortified one day with this vast store of ignorance, I plunged confidently into learning all there was to know about our new computer system. The euphoria lasted 10 minutes, tops. The darned thing seized and adamantly refused to answer my commands. What nerve!

"Carrie!" I called out to our 14-year-old, the only offspring with the misfortune of being home at the time. Our three daughters then ranged from early teen to adolescent. (Yeah, three teenaged girls. Well, that's a story for another time.)

"Yes Dad?" I heard her answer from her room.

"This goddamned thing is frozen!" I said, loud enough that neighbors even a few doors away could hear.

"Harrumph!" came the sound of my wife, admonishing me for my strong language.

On such occasions, she'd clear her throat in that subtle way, just for me. "Harrumph!" She was mercifully reluctant to undertake in front of our kids the behavior modification of which her spouse was in such desperate need. Thus, the throat clearing came to be 'the signal' that I'd egregiously transgressed certain verbal boundaries. There must have been times when she had the clearest throat on the planet.

"Be right there Dad," Carrie said, undaunted by my detour into the blue nether land of the English lexicon.

On arrival at the den, she declined my invitation to sit at the desk, implying this would take no time at all. It didn't. She leaned over the keyboard and with a few quick strokes I was back in business.

"How'd you do that?" I asked, flabbergasted.

"It's okay, Dad," Carrie replied, trying not to betray impatience with her parent. "Just don't do... "

I had no idea what she had just said. And the darned kid was quick to pick up on the bewildered look in my eyes.

"Just call me if you get stuck again," Carrie said, showing remarkable restraint for her young age. I understood the message: she was putting herself on standby. Good thing as it turned out.

On many subsequent visits, Carrie rescued me from computer purgatory. It took her almost no time at all. She'd spend much more time browsing our wall of books, evidently attracted to the knowledge lurking within. Books were my thing and to my joy they were becoming hers too, apparently. Her interest warmed the cockles of my heart. As it turned out, her attraction to books would be at the core of a family mystery soon to unfold.

The books in our den included a few textbooks from my courses while at university. Among these were works by great thinkers like Aristotle, Socrates and Plato. I was quite fond of Plato, or rather of what little I understood. I kept these works hoping that one day I'd actually find time to read and perhaps even understand them. Good luck with that!

One day, while at work in the den my intuition signaled that something was not right. There was a gap in the meticulous lineup of books on one shelf. A book was missing! Most puzzling of all, the absent book turned out to be Plato. Until then, no one else had shown even a passing interest in any of the books, much less works of the great Greek philosophers.

The errant Plato's The Republic remained an enigma for weeks. After checking high and low with a sense of mission, it was nowhere to be found. I was certain of two things: first, I'd not taken the book somewhere to read, and, two, no one in the family had shown any interest in Plato.

Well, I was right on the first and wrong on the second.

One weekend, while engaged in some handyman work around the house my wife called sweetly to ask a big favor. That sweet tone is never a good sign, as husbands everywhere know full well.

"Honey, will you go and collect all of the dirty dishes for me from Carrie's room?"

It was common knowledge among our family and friends that my wife refused to go anywhere near Carrie's notoriously unkept domain. Now, anyone with the courage of Crocodile Dundee and a willingness to venture into that repository of unimaginable chaos learned immediately the harsh realities of coming face-to-face with grave personal danger.

Within minutes my arms were loaded down with kitchen dishes. To each adhered the remnants of objects hinting they were once edible, sometime during past days, weeks, perhaps even months. All now resembled fossils at varying stages of petrification.

And then, Hallelujah!

Under a plate loaded with the gastronomic detritus of times past, there it was: The Republic of Plato, in all of its wondrous splendor!

Later, naturally, Carrie and I spoke of Plato, and to a lesser extent about how it came to pass that Plato had made a pilgrimage from our den to her chaotic boudoir. Seems Plato’s tome had caught her eye and raised her curiosity on one of her frequent missions to rescue her father from the vicissitudes of an obstinate and unforgiving computer. And I’ll be darned if she wasn’t also able to explain some of Plato to me, too. Smart kid, twice over.

Fourteen years old. I’ll be damned!

Harrumph!

The Darrin Chronicles

Darrin was 2½ when he decided to help his grandfather build a bedroom in the basement of his parents' home. Right after breakfast, off he went to work downstairs, properly equipped with a fresh diaper. He found his grandfather at work on the basement bedroom.

"Are you working today, Grandpa?" Darrin asked rhetorically, pudgy little hands tucked in the back pockets of tiny blue jeans. The pockets were the size of postage stamps.

"Yes, Darrin," Grandpa replied, surveying the drywall he'd finished installing the day before. "Time to get these walls ready for painting. Would you like to go upstairs and get your tools?"

Darrin's dark brown eyes sparkled. An ear-to-ear grin lit up his cherubic face.

Up the stairs on all four, Darrin scrambled to his bedroom on the second floor. There, he donned his clear plastic see-through 'Bob The Builder' backpack filled with his construction tools. With his bright yellow 'hard hat' set firmly on his head, Darrin headed downstairs, reaching up for the handrail to steady his descent.

Back in the basement, off came the backpack. Darrin unzipped the flap. Out poured his entire collection of plastic tools: a red screwdriver, a hammer with a blue handle and yellow head, a bright yellow ruler. Oh, also there was a #2 Phillips screwdriver he'd appropriated a few weeks earlier from his Grandpa's toolbox. Darrin was ready for work.

"Today," Grandpa said, "We're going to apply the first coat of plaster to the nail holes and seams in the drywall."

Darrin had no idea with his grandpa had just said. Regardless, with his help the job took at least twice as long as expected. Among other reasons, Darrin kept losing from his feet one or both of his Grandpa's old runners that he insisted on wearing. After all, he'd seen Grandpa put on his 'work shoes'.

Work progressed. Then, while his Grandpa's attention was elsewhere briefly, Darrin dug a trowel into a bucket of wet plaster. At that point, what else was Grandpa to do but let Darrin smear it on the walls just like he'd watched grandfather do it (more or less)?

"This is fun!" Darrin said.

He proved it by taking much longer than the usual two to five minutes to lose interest in the task at hand.

Darrin could reach up only about 40 inches, and that was a good thing. Otherwise, Grandpa would have had a much larger area of wall to scrape and to sand, so that it would be ready once more for painting.

The novelty did finally wear off. Darrin decided to end that chapter of the Great Plaster Caper when plaster sticking to his hands began to dry. His wrinkled nose and look of apprehension convinced Grandpa to take Darrin into the bathroom and wash his hands. That done, Darrin was suddenly overcome by a compelling need to go find his dog Jackson.

But the Great Plaster Caper didn't end there. Nor, did wee Darrin's influence. Some lessons flowed from that episode and parallel episodes earlier and later. Among them:

1. When sanding drywall plaster on ceilings, the least accessible nook or cranny can be sanded only by using those muscles already sore and tired from showing your grandchild how it's done. This comes partly from scrambling up and down stepladders carrying your grandchild to show him up close how it's coming along.
2. Within a very short time after starting to sand the ceiling, it becomes readily apparent that abhorrent chores like changing soiled diapers or even fixing

barbed wire fences would be cause for celebration by comparison.

3. While taking breaks, it's always wise to remove one's dust-encrusted particle mask before attempting to take a sip from that forgotten and now cold cup of coffee, covered with a scum of plaster dust – the same one into which your grandchild earlier dipped his plaster trowel.
4. While sweeping up the dust after a round of sanding, with your grandchild on hands and knees trying hard to assist, the furnace or air conditioner will come on, making sure to spread the product of your labors throughout the house. It will not matter that you attempted to seal off the room with sheets of plastic. Your grandchild will have experimented vigorously with the integrity of the seal, inevitably tearing it from its moorings.
5. Once you've concluded (foolishly) that you are done and ready to start painting, you will do some 'finish sanding' on the occasional visible blemish. Naturally, just as you are concluding that light gentle sanding, something long, black and resembling a thread or horsehair (horsehair?) will pop out at you. Also, naturally, you will tug on it to remove this shocking blemish, whereupon large chunks of plaster will give way along with the offending debris. At first glance, the gash resulting will look big enough to park a railway locomotive – well, okay, not quite. This is when you invite your grandchild's mother (okay, you beg her) to recover her offspring. Whereupon, in your solitude you utter a quiet prayer... well, it kinda sounds like a prayer. Some of the words are similar.
6. Once you have concluded again (also foolishly) that you are done, you will step back to survey your accomplishment. You will view your job with

satisfaction and a wee bit of smugness. However, while backing up further, you will step on an errant screwdriver left behind by that wonderful grandchild. This will cause you to loose balance and fall back heavily, crashing into the wall behind you. That's when you discover a sharp plaster trowel you forgot in you back pocket is now imbedded in the wall. You utter more words that have a similarity to prayer.

7. You will conclude once again... and even more foolishly... that you are done. Whereupon you will shower thoroughly, purge all exposed orifices (surely there's a more genteel description), and dress in a complete change of clean clothes head to toe. All done, right? Not so fast! The very first dark colored item you come anywhere near will promptly reveal white, dusty evidence of your passage. T'was ever thus.

Mrs. George

By almost any measure you could think of, Mrs. George was eccentric.

Maybe it was her hair, dyed the color of the setting sun. Or perhaps it was catching a whiff of her breath, seasoned with drops of perfume. Or it could have been her unusual home, decorated whimsically with a seemingly random collection of relics from bygone glories.

Regardless, all who came within range of this charming 80-something woman succumbed to the alluring intelligence in her sparkling eyes. Those hazel eyes spoke eloquently of a kind heart, of practical wisdom earned from a life fully embraced, and of an energetic sense of humor promising to erupt on a moment's notice.

Home was a long, narrow apartment tucked under the wing of a downtown theatre building, perhaps even older than this warm-hearted octogenarian. Her front door was easily missed, stuck in the shade of a pilaster on the building's facade, six steps to the right of the theatre's main entrance.

Judi was the architect of my first encounter with Mrs. George – I never knew her by any other name. She was a revelation to a naive young man in his early 20s. Her clothing of preference, shapeless housedresses decorated with bright floral patterns, was outshone by a huge smile accented with brilliant red lipstick.

Quite possibly it was the clatter of her loose-fitting dentures that kept her mindful of her breath, which I learned later she sweetened with drops of perfume placed under her tongue, timed strategically to make the best use of it.

So it was no surprise that this kindly lady was an incurable romantic, harboring a generous soft spot in her heart for young lovers. It's a good thing that she did. Her wonderful nature would have a lasting influence on the rest of my life.

*

A few weeks earlier, Judi and I had met at work. Okay, full disclosure: the very moment I saw her arrive for her first day of work, this incontrovertibly and adamantly confirmed bachelor was suddenly and hopelessly in love.

"I'm staying with a friend of my aunt," Judi said one Friday night after an office curling league game. She had reluctantly agreed to go for coffee after the game, the only concession resembling a date I'd been granted thus far. I was looking forward eagerly to being allowed to drive her home. She lived an hour out of town and commuted to work with her uncle. Had my wish of wishes been granted, we would have actually been able to spend that hour alone together. Good luck with that!

"Her name's Mrs. George," Judi had said. "She has a little apartment. I sleep on her couch the nights we have a game."

I wouldn't meet Mrs. George for a while. Judi had agreed that after coffee I could drive her to the theatre building, and drop her off out front. Weeks later our relationship took a huge step forward – one night I was allowed to arrive at Mrs. George's apartment, pick up Judi and drive her to the curling rink.

That night I arrived at the door, feeling apprehensive. It opened. Mrs. George's smile lit up the doorway. She ushered me in. I followed her and the haze of perfume that enveloped her short abundant frame down a narrow hallway to her tiny living room. Her small talk en route left no doubt that she understood the urgencies of young love, and that she approved wholeheartedly of the concept.

"Sit!" she said. Her command was pointed, her tone kindly. "She'll be right out."

I managed a quick glance around while surrendering as ordered into the deep embrace of an overstuffed armchair, a throwback to a bygone era. The living room was crowded with rich-looking furniture, and a collection of artwork and artifacts worthy of envy by almost any a museum curator.

Mrs. George took three steps across the narrow living room and sat on a matching sofa, facing me. She looked squarely into my eyes. Her gaze was searching and intense while also kindly. Disarming. She asked questions about my job, my family, my hometown, and my future – all in a friendly conversational manner. I realized later she was checking me out on behalf of her pretty young charge I'd come to date.

Someone once described a person's physical stature as being built like a fire hydrant. Mrs. George could have been the template, but in fairness we'll just say she was well upholstered. The details of her physical secrets were secure beneath those paisley floral housedresses, each of which bore evidence of having been mended repeatedly with a dizzying array of mismatched colored threads. And despite both her unconventional appearance and being vertically challenged she had that rare ability to command attention, unintentionally most of the time.

That evening, when she'd sat across from me, the hem of her floor-length dress had risen ever so slightly, revealing black silk slippers decorated with multi-colored beads arranged in bright floral patterns (what else?), and flesh-colored hose rolled down to tiny ankles revealing pale skin the texture of parchment.

"Ready to go?" Judi asked. Mrs. George rose quickly to her feet.

She reached out to give Judi a hug, then turned to me. I found myself promptly enveloped into that perfume haze where she lived.

*

Mrs. George mercifully was discreet. She never told on us, nor ever said a word when Judi arrived very late, or very early the next morning, and sometimes not at all. We were engaged by then, but her overly protective uncle could have posed a problem, or her mother Edith would have bestowed choice words upon her eldest daughter, and upon me.

We last laid eyes on the redoubtable Mrs. George while making our way back down the aisle after being married. There she was, sitting in a pew next to the aisle, resplendent in a new royal blue dress. Okay, it was nearly new – one button was attached with a different colored thread.

*

A few years later and thousands of miles away, we learned that Mrs. George had passed away. We were sad, of course, but also happy and grateful for the privilege of having known her.

Her legacy? Mrs. George set a life example that all of us would do well to emulate.

Skydiving The Bucket List

The panic lasted a nanosecond. Suddenly, the door of the tiny aircraft slammed up and open. We were at 10,000 feet. Time to jump.

The slipstream screamed past the open door. It was fierce.

My daughter went first. Kim said something I couldn't hear. She admitted later that she mouthed an unladylike expletive while pausing briefly at the edge of the open door, her eyes wide. Then she jumped. Amazing. I was so proud.

An hour earlier, our family had gathered at the airfield. Quite a group had assembled to witness this 'bucket list' jump for my 70th birthday: four daughters, their spouses/partners, families and friends. In all, nine grandchildren and twelve adults.

Before jumping, I was required to visit the front desk of the skydiving club and sign the usual legal disclaimer: 'my survivors will not sue you'. Then I paid. The fee would allow me to jump out of a perfectly good aircraft. *Am I nuts?* I was thinking just as Kim walked up and astounded me with: "Dad, what would you think if I jumped, too?"

I didn't take her seriously, at first. She had enough on her plate – a nasty divorce, getting settled in new surroundings, a challenging job and a new relationship with a man also dealing with an acrimonious divorce... quite enough, already. Besides, she suffers from vertigo! I was concerned – mistakenly – she might loose heart at the last minute and embarrass herself. As it turned out, I'm the one who was embarrassed... for under-estimating my daughter.

That little lady proved to her family and friends, and most importantly to herself, she's made of sterner stuff than I'd credited her with.

So there we were at 10,000 feet (almost two miles

high) looking for patches of blue in an otherwise overcast and rainy sky. Suddenly, the pilot of the single-engine Cessna pops up the door. Kim was beside the void left by the door. Out she went. Then me.

By the time I was airborne Kim was a distant speck against light gray billowy clouds.

We got to free-fall for the first 5,000 feet. Skydivers in free-fall reach terminal velocity – that's 124 miles an hour (200 km an hour) – in the blink of an eye.

At first, we fell in a big arc forward and down, and then straight down. Fast!

The experience is beyond mere words to describe.

There's almost no sense of falling.

Except for the rushing air.

And flapping clothes... And flapping cheeks... don't even try to grin.

You look around. There are no reference points.

No way to gauge the speed of your downward movement... up there.

No trees or tall buildings, or power poles... to judge speed... and progress... as you go down! Fast! Very fast!

Nor are there many birds up that high, either.

And looking straight down from that height you have almost no sensation you're hurtling toward the ground at terminal velocity. Besides, you're much too busy, overwhelmed with the magnificent vistas all around you.

The feeling of freedom is exhilarating.

This is what it's like to get high on being high!

There are no apparent encumbrances.

Even the cushion of air slowing your downward progress feels friendly.

The power of gravity must have been turned off... for the moment.

Except that constant reminder... air screaming past your ears.

You notice the view again. It's beyond spectacular.

And there are no airplane windows in the way... or anything else.

You look around 360 degrees at all the magnificent mountains, lakes, rivers, golf courses, towns, roads and farms. The colors are stunning... multitudinous shades of greens in the forests and orchards and fields, and the countless hues of blue and aquamarine in the lakes and rivers and creeks.

The roar of the air blots out almost all sounds except itself.

I tweak my outstretched fingers just slightly, like I'd been shown.

The influence on the rushing air is enough to cause a spin. Tweaking my fingers the other way reverses the spin. Amazing! What an extraordinary experience! I do it again, and again. Fun!

Kim's blue parachute pops open below, to the left. She's maybe 1,500 to 2,000 feet down.

It signals our free-fall is over... much too soon! I'm disappointed.

Then my bright red parachute snaps open. The harness grabs hard at legs and arms. We've dropped 5,000 feet (1½ kilometers) far too quickly. Yes, it is disappointing... but yes the tug of those straps is also reassuring. The ground below has suddenly become surprisingly close

I grab the handles of my parachute and turn in a wide sweeping 360-degree circle. Then I pull hard on the left handle and raise the right, swinging back in a huge arc. What an extraordinary experience. I don't want to stop. It's no wonder birds enjoy being birds so much. Well, they seem that way early most mornings.

With the parachute open, sounds can be heard again.

Daughter Kim is just below me, still squealing happily. She screams in delight all the way down to a landing precisely on the 'X" made of white canvas strips on the ground. Unfortunately, she injured her ankle slightly. So caught up in the thrill of the experience she forgot the tandem instructor's directions to raise her feet and look at the horizon while landing.

Yeah, we're novices. We were obliged to jump with instructors. Well worth it anyway. They added knowledge and technique to the jump that comes only with much experience.

The jump may have been on my 'bucket list' for turning 70, but the thrill of skydiving with daughter Kim cranked that experience way up a whole bunch of notches.

And as Kim put it after her jump:

"Now, there's nothing I can't do."

I believe her.

Getting Rowdy

The neighborhood missed him and his family when they moved to the country. But Keith and his wife Elsabeth wanted their children to enjoy the rural lifestyle.

Their ranch-style house on the acreage offered a commanding view of the surrounding countryside. It sat atop a high peninsula of land and soon was joined by a modern barn containing four stalls, a work area and a large hayloft.

The acreage became a haven for Keith. He led a busy life as a successful businessman, entrepreneur and community volunteer. He found welcome relaxation in the evenings caring for their horses, dogs, cats, plus an adoption that Keith didn't expect or want... at first.

It wasn't the only surprises he and visitors to the acreage were to encounter.

Strangers would often arrive and cower fearfully in their cars... having been greeted by Bosley, an enormous Bouvier dog, and Sheba, an equally big Sheepdog. The two dogs loved to bound along, one on each side of arriving cars, barking loudly. Their huge faces – seemingly the size of buffalo heads – would bob along, level with the car windows as they peered in.

Most strangers refused to leave their vehicles until Keith or another family member rescued them. Some arriving strangers simply backed their vehicles out of the yard and drove away. Keith suspected they were selling something. Good riddance.

None could know what friends knew – that Bosley and Sheba had the personalities of affectionate teddy bears. They'd happily accept a scratch behind their ears, rather than bite someone, every single time... coyotes and other predators excepted.

Their successor, Oliver, was an unusually tall male Boxer. The family adopted him as a puppy. From the start, his favorite place was on someone's lap. It calmed the fears of a frightened little puppy.

Oliver grew up into an oversized but still-affectionate Boxer. And he never forgot his favorite place. The family got used to chasing Oliver off their laps, much to Oliver's disappointment. Some visitors didn't know about Oliver's annoying habit, just yet.

One day, their friend Judi came to visit. She liked dogs, and had known Oliver from a puppy. And Oliver, now all grown up, loved petite little Judi. Predictably, one day while Judi was sitting on the couch and wasn't looking, Oliver jumped onto her lap. Judi all but disappeared behind Oliver's hulking body. She had to be rescued by Keith.

And then there was Rowdy, the goat.

Keith's children had a great sense of humor. That's how Rowdy arrived – as a baby Billie goat, a.k.a., a kid. It was their idea of a fun birthday present for their dad. He didn't share their humor with quite the same enthusiasm.

It didn't take long for the rambunctious bovid to earn his name.

Eventually, Keith and Rowdy developed a rapport, of sorts. Perhaps it was their similar personalities. Keith was strong willed and so was the aptly named Rowdy. The problem was, Rowdy seemed oblivious to what others thought about him. He did whatever he pleased, despite Keith's best efforts at training him to behave. Perhaps the two were more alike than Keith cared to admit.

Rowdy hung out mostly in the barn, or more accurately, it became his domain. When not lording it over horses, cats, dogs and other creatures that he deemed to be under his jurisdiction, Rowdy could be found raiding the garden, or chomping on everything from fence rails to tin cans... or he'd be dining out on Elsabeth's newly planted flowers, shrubs and trees.

Regardless of what Keith might have thought about his white-coated pet, Rowdy developed a strong affection for him. (We have it on good authority Keith liked Rowdy, too, grudgingly, but didn't want anyone to know.)

Rowdy had been only a few months old when he adopted the practice of being inside the barn, waiting behind the door, when Keith arrived to feed the animals. Rowdy would follow Keith everywhere, staying hard on his heels as Keith went about the chores.

One day, Keith was preparing to feed his horses when he heard Rowdy making plaintive noises. For once, Rowdy wasn't at his heels. When Keith looked around there was no sign of the little white Billie goat. Keith scoured the stalls in the barn. He even climbed up into the hayloft, certain that Rowdy couldn't possibly get up there... but not entirely certain. Keith searched the yard outside again and again. Rowdy was nowhere to be found. But he could still hear Rowdy's muted cries of distress.

Keith went back inside, again walking through the stalls and work area, looking around carefully. The cries were louder. Stopping to listen more intently, he leaned on a 45-gallon drum half filled with feed grain.

One side of the hand-made wooden top gave way beneath his elbow and flipped. The edge almost smacked the head of a frightened Rowdy, his feet sunk deep in the feed grain. He looked up at his owner, pleading with soulful eyes. Rowdy wanted out, and he wasn't kidding.

When Keith stopped laughing, he concluded Rowdy must have jumped onto the lid while his back was turned, trying to get closer to him, and flipped it, throwing himself down into the barrel. His feet had become mired in the feed grain making it impossible for him to climb back out.

Rowdy remained full of mischief for the rest of his life, but he never tried that again.

Healing Energy

A True Story

Chayton was visiting his grandmother one afternoon when he developed a stomachache.

"Let's make a healing energy ball," she said, wanting to soothe her four-year-old grandson's discomfort.

She held her hands cupped one above the other, at first facing each other, and then side by side, and then in different directions.

Chayton watched her hands move gently around and around, and in and out, making an imaginary ball. Her hands moved as if kneading invisible bread dough, except this was very different.

"I can feel the healing energy and it's glowing," his grandmother said calmly, a loving smile on her radiant face. "It's bright green, like the color of the earth."

She slowly eased her cupped hands a few inches towards him.

"The energy wants to come to you," she said. "May I let it enter your tummy?" she asked, moving her hands closer to his midsection. "This'll make it all better."

Chayton nodded, his trusting eyes fixed on his grandmother.

Then her cupped hands edged gently closer, as if presenting the invisible 'energy ball' to his stomach for it to embrace. He watched each of her moves closely, wide-eyed. His face showed wonder and apprehension mixed with skepticism.

Chayton went home happy that day, the pain of his stomachache evidently gone. He didn't complain about it, at least.

A few weeks after his stomachache episode, Chayton was home with his mother. Tam's a single parent. She was struggling with a promising relationship. Most adults will have experienced these struggles. As we all know they can be emotionally painful. This was no exception.

One afternoon, Chayton came into Tam's home office expecting to find her at work as usual. He found his mother at her desk in tears. She quickly regained her composure, but Chayton noticed.

A few hours later they were in the living room playing a game just before supper. Chayton could see his mother was still unhappy.

He walked over and stood in front of her, forming his hands into an 'energy ball' as his grandmother had shown him. Chayton stretched his little arms out towards her heart, his hands cupped, saying: "Here Mommy, this healing energy ball will make your heart happy again."

And so it did.

Sleeping Over

Their parents agreed one weekend that Rick could sleep over at his friend Nick's house. Two miles separated their farms. The boys were seven. It would be their first sleepover... and their last.

Nick's mother was a warm, kind-hearted soul who spoke little English. No need. The smiles that danced in her sparkling blue-green eyes spoke volumes. She and Nick's Dad had emigrated from Ukraine many years earlier.

Over supper, she encouraged Rick to learn a few words of Ukrainian. They coincided with the English words for common expressions like 'hello' and 'goodbye', 'good morning' and 'good night', and table items like 'knife', 'fork' and 'spoon'.

Rick found it interesting and fun to learn a little bit about another language. He concentrated hard, trying to remember and worked hard learning to pronounce words that were awkward to his tongue. He wanted very much to please Nick's Mom.

Later that evening, after the boys went upstairs to bed, Nick generously offered to teach Tommy more Ukrainian words. He was like that. Rick agreed eagerly. They worked at it until Nick's mother called sternly for them to quiet down for the night.

The next morning, Rick got his first opportunity to show off his newly learned Ukrainian words. Drawn to Nick's mother's kindly nature, he wanted to please her. So, when Mike and Rick walked into the kitchen Rick greeted her, as best as he could remember and pronounce, with one of the phrases she'd taught him during supper. Before coming down, Mike had rehearsed him again how to say, "Good Morning!" in Ukrainian. As soon as he said it, her face lit up with a beaming smile. Tommy was so proud! She warmly replied: "Ласкаво Ранок!"

That confirmed she was pleased with his efforts,

and was impressed. Rick was delighted that he'd pleased her.

The two boys sat down for breakfast at the kitchen table. It was Sunday morning and the family was assembled: Nick's parents, his two sisters, one brother... and the two of them. It was obvious where Nick had come by his engaging smile – his Dad also sported a massive beaming smile. His Dad's perpetually happy face lit up a room wherever he went.

Encouraged by Nick and his Mom, Rick was eager to show off even more, and to please everyone with his newfound grasp of Ukrainian.

Rick picked up the glass of fresh milk where he was sitting and promptly rhymed off the words for the milk and the glass that Mike had taught him the night before, and then carefully coached him again in the morning.

At that moment, Nick's mother happened to be holding a huge cast iron frying pan filled with scrambled eggs. It crashed down onto the massive wood-fired cook stove. Her eyes widened and her mouth opened, speechless. A stern expression came over his father's face, but he couldn't hide the laughter in his eyes. His brother made no such effort. He burst out laughing. Nick's sisters seemed undecided whether to laugh or feign shock. They turned away.

Nick's mother pointed her finger sternly at Nick and then toward the door from the kitchen leading upstairs. Nick slinked out, presumably up to his room, where his dastardly plot had been hatched the night before.

Within minutes, Rick was heading down the gravel road toward his home two miles away... alone and without breakfast.

Eventually, Rick learned the meaning of the Ukrainian words Nick had taught him. When translated into English they included the f-bomb, that 'mother' of all profane four-letter words.

Oops.

The boys remained friends and like most youngsters growing up as friends, they chalked up many an adventure. Some they got into on their own and others by watching the bigger boys at school ‘do exciting things’, that is, whenever the big boys would let them hang around.

One day, the two were bicycling home together from school. They came to the top of a hill and saw a group of big boys standing around a small fire of twigs and dead grass in the middle of the gravel road. They were throwing stuff into it.

“Let’s go see what they’re doing,” Rick said. The two boys put their bikes down and walked over. They stood back, wondering what was going on.

The big boys kept throwing shiny things into the fire. All of a sudden, there was a loud ‘pop’ from the fire and Rick’s right earlobe started to sting. He felt like his earlobe was being squeezed with pliers.

“Ouch!” he said, grabbing his earlobe. “That hurt! I think a bee stung me, or a black fly bit me!”

The big boys were laughing at the ‘pop’. They didn’t know Rick was hurt.

“Come have a look,” Rick asked Nick. He kept grabbing at his right earlobe. Nick took one look and his eyes flew open wide.

“You’re bleeding!” he yelled. He pulled Rick toward their bikes. They hopped on. Nick watched his friend all the way home. Rick’s mother was upset. She did the first aid thing. She was used to it by now. Nick stood there deeply concerned.

Rick didn’t know then what had happened. Nick thought he did. He feared Rick had been shot. Nick had recognized what the big boys had been throwing into the fire—.22-caliber rifle shells, then waiting for them explode.

When Nick told her that, Rick’s mother was furious. The hot shell casing of one had hit Rick’s earlobe after exploding in the fire. The bullet, the lead part of the shell, was much heavier and had stayed behind in the fire. The damage was minor. And any real danger was less than negligible. Truth was, Rick did most of the damage by pulling and scratching his earlobe, causing a blister formed by the hot shell casing to bleed a little.

Yup, boys are destined to be boys!

Anchors Away

New boat owners endure a multitude of experiences while climbing steep learning curves. Some of those lessons are basic, some are humorous and some are frustrating... all are expensive. Tom and Susan were no exception.

It was spring and they'd taken possession of their 25-foot sleep-aboard cruiser late the previous summer. The original owner had retired and moved away. Perfect!

Well almost.

They soon realized to their dismay the accessories that normally outfit a boat were missing – life jackets, paddles, dock lines; galley provisions like pots, pans, dishes, cutlery; essentials for the 'head' (toilet). Even a fish finder/depth gauge had been removed, the mounting bracket left behind for some inexplicable reason; similarly with a floodlight, the bracket and light gone, leaving behind four ugly screw holes in the hull.

Then the last straw: the anchor was gone, as well as the anchor line (that's 'rope' in sailor talk).

In their naiveté, they'd failed to notice the missing provisions and so had not insisted these be included in the deal. Replacement costs would ultimately exceed several thousand dollars. They accused the salesman of stripping the boat before selling it for the previous owner on consignment. He denied it of course, unconvincingly. And then, that unrepentant bandit had the gall to offer them "one hell of a deal" on replacements for the missing provisions.

Some of the items were legal requirements: life jackets, paddles (tho' who in the world's going to paddle a 25-foot boat anywhere?), and of course, an anchor.

They were anxious to start using their boat. Reluctantly they purchased the legal essentials from that snake oil salesman: life jackets, paddles, anchor, and dock lines. Oh yes, and toilet paper and holding tank chemicals for the head.

Now, at this point, they knew nothing about anchors. They bought a mid-priced model. Turned out it was much too small. And they purchased 75 feet of anchor line. Turned out it was much too short. They didn't know at the time the lake is close to 450 feet deep in the middle; even many of the bays are 100 feet deep.

Another lesson learned: seek advice only from those who know what they're talking about.

Legally outfitted, off they went exploring 'their' picturesque lake, some 70 miles long and averaging five miles wide. They burned through more tanks of gas than they cared to admit while discovering the extraordinary beauty of the lake, and a few sheltered bays that would soon become favorite places for them to anchor overnight.

As time went by, they learned more about the boat and how to provision it properly. The shopping list seemed never to get any shorter. There is much truth to the saying: a boat is a hole in the water into which the owner pours money.

One essential soon became obvious: they needed to replace the too-small anchor they'd purchased and its too-short anchor line. An undersized anchor just wouldn't do. And they were cautioned that a sailor does not tie a piece of rope onto an existing line. With wave action they often part, sometimes in the middle of the night. That's not surprising; when fully provisioned with 400 gallons of gas and 45 gallons of water the boat weighed more than 2½ tons. They realized that to keep from losing the boat in a high wind, they needed something fairly big that would stick firmly into the lake bottom, and be attached to a sturdy one-piece line.

With the advice of experienced sailors, they purchased a big double-fluke anchor (that's boater talk), 150 feet of half-inch nylon anchor line and 20 feet of anchor chain. The new stuff almost filled the anchor locker in the bow of the boat.

Thus equipped, they were looking forward to a weekend of on-board camping. Before leaving, Tom had attached with great care the new anchor to the anchor chain and then the chain to the new line. He followed the explicit instructions of those more experienced in these matters. They explained the chain would ensure the anchor came to rest on its side on the lake bottom and thus more likely to dig in properly. Made sense.

Tom and Susan loaded the boat up with food, drink and other essentials, and headed out. It was a beautiful Friday afternoon. All signs pointed to a weekend of spectacular weather.

They arrived in mid-afternoon at one of their favorite bays. There was plenty of time to get settled before supper. They were delighted to be the first in the bay; they had their choice of locations.

First, they needed to anchor. Tom went to the bow and opened the anchor locker. He couldn't wait to deploy the new anchor assembly. They knew the water in that bay could be up to 75 feet deep close to shore, and deeper farther out. The lake bottom dropped sharply even farther not far from the bay. No problem. They'd be fine.

Tom threw the shiny new double-fluke anchor overboard. Then he watched as the glistening pristine line went zipping through the polished chrome guide on the bow, the assembly engaged in its first assignment.

And then, along came one of those "Oh Shit!" moments!

He remembered something; he'd forgot to secure the other end of the anchor line. A grab for it was too late. Tom watched as the end of the rope shot over the side, and disappeared below the surface of the water.

Susan and Tom looked at each other, shook their heads and burst out laughing. What else? One more step up the learning curve. Sigh!

Unable to anchor and unwilling to end their weekend before it had started, they found another bay. Some kind-hearted soul had installed a dock where they could tie up.

Pantomime Hunter

Michael was a quiet kid in elementary school. His teachers decided he was shy. They were in for a shock.

Being dutiful pedagogists, the teachers agreed they had an obligation to help this unfortunate youngster overcome his debilitating 'social handicap'. Their solution was to place Michael in situations requiring him to 'express himself'.

One of these came up in his English class. The students were learning forms of dramatic expression that they would find in literature and film, and on stage and TV. Their teacher, an aspiring thespian, decided the students could learn best by actually performing the art forms. She decided to start with pantomime, and was confident that it would also provide excellent therapeutic therapy for Michael.

The students were instructed to discuss with their parents a subject from their lives they could perform in pantomime form, and then prepare a script. As a fun twist on the exercise, each student would perform their pantomime solo without telling his or her classmates what it was about. Their fellow students would be challenged to guess the subject.

That's where the fun began.

Like his parents, Michael was blessed with a creative mind and a wicked sense of humor. His teachers were mistaken – while Michael was quiet, he was anything but shy.

One evening over supper, as the date of the students' pantomime performances drew near, Michael, his parents and his sister thought hard about a subject for his performance.

"Remember our duck hunting trip a few weeks ago?" his Dad said. "Why don't you play a duck hunter?"

"Great idea, Dad!" Michael said.

He remembered going hunting with his Dad. It had been early one morning. He was too young to use a gun and was kept a safe distance from the shooting. Before then, he was allowed close enough to watch his Dad and fellow hunters build a hunting blind. And he watched attentively as they built and used a latrine complete with a privacy screen made from bushes, and a log to sit on when needed... for the bigger jobs. Hey, the wait times while hunting can go on for hours.

Michael's father coached him with his script, describing the hunters' experiences in the blind, and the need to act quickly when ducks flew past within range. That evening, Michael applied his creative mind to his script. And that's where his wicked sense of humor kicked in. The teachers got one version of his script; he had another scenario in mind. Michael's version had to do with a hunter seated in the latrine being called upon to make a hasty response to an incoming flock of ducks.

The day of the performances arrived. Michael's turn came.

He walked to the front of the classroom. A gym bag was clutched in his hand. From it he extracted an outfit he'd gathered from his Dad's hunting clothes, including a reflective red jacket much too large and a red felt hat that teetered on his ears. Michael also carried a long stick, to serve as his fake shotgun. (It wasn't easy getting the stick into the school. His teacher had to intervene.)

Before he'd finished dressing, Michael's audience of fellow students began guessing his pantomime subject. A barrage of shouted guesses erupted. He shook his head, 'no' to all of them.

First, he pantomimed building a hunting blind, and then a latrine. Then came gestures resembling a boy relieving himself. The teachers raised their eyebrows. Then, Michael shaded his eyes and cast his gaze across the classroom, as if looking for incoming ducks.

Once more, the other kids began shouting out their answers. Again, Michael nodded 'no'.

To the chagrin of his teachers, Michael suddenly put his hand over the back of his pants as if overcome by an urgent need to use the toilet. Fake gun in hand, he scampered to the location on stage where he'd pantomimed building a latrine. He pretended to lower his pants, and then squatted. He placed his fake gun/stick across his knees.

By now, his fellow students were beside themselves with laughter. And by now, his teachers' attitudes had gone from mild concern to serious worry.

Michael put his hand out. In it he was holding a real piece of paper. Its purpose was to portray toilet paper. He reached back behind his rear end and pantomimed the well-known act of wiping himself.

While squatting, his other hand went to his ear, and then he shaded his eyes. The message: ducks were coming, and coming fast. His fake gun was balanced across his knees.

He jumped up, holding the fake gun in one hand. Then he looked puzzled. What to do? His other hand held the paper. As if by instinct, he raised the faux toilet paper and grabbed it with his mouth. Then he proceeded to pantomime shooting make-believe ducks flying past.

Michael's fellow students were doubled over helpless with laughter. His teachers were struggling to keep straight faces. They failed.

Never again was Michael considered shy.

Author's Note: 'The Pantomime Hunter' was inspired by a true story. Today, Michael is a successful engineer, married with two children, and still enjoys a wicked sense of humor.

The Elbow Follies

Elbow Falls is a long way up a tree-lined valley in the Rocky Mountains. Hiking trails are plentiful. But spring flooding on the Elbow River can make changes to the valley, including trails that catch visitors unaware. That's just what happened to a pair of venturesome hikers one day.

Alan and Sherry were new to being a couple... and they were enjoying it more and more. Both were middle aged and single. They'd discovered hiking was among their many shared interests, much to their delight. One afternoon, they set out from a trailhead at Elbow Falls, hiking downstream along the top edge of the steep tree-covered valley, 200 feet above the river.

"There's a great little beach I'd like you to see," Alan said. "It's on a bend in the river downstream... not far from here. This trail should get us there"

He was remembering a visit a few years earlier, and the hike down to the river shore. Sherry also remembered hiking in the area. Their chosen trail began to angle downwards. It came to a 'Y'. One branch went back up and one seemed inclined to go down. They headed down.

Half way to the valley floor, the trail suddenly ended. A large section of bank had slid down to the river, now 100 feet below. Spring floodwaters had poured over the bank from the mountain valley behind, causing a landslide.

The disappointed twosome looked at each other. They discussed options and agreed their hike should not end like this. Both were wearing sturdy footwear.

"We can always take the lower trail back up," Alan said. "You know, the other one we were thinking about taking."

Sherry remembered that trail and nodded, feeling reassured. They'd rejected it as less interesting in favor of this one.

"Okay," she said gamely. "Let's work our way down."

Grabbing onto shrubs and small trees on the edge of the washout, they began gradually making their way towards the river. To their dismay, halfway there the shrubs and trees ended. It was too steep to go back easily. The bank was dry. So giggling like elementary school kids they sat down on the loose dirt and slid down to the shore of the glacier-fed river.

When they came to a stop their feet were within inches of a sharp drop they'd not to seen from above. Ten feet directly below was the ice-cold turbulent river, eight to 10 feet deep.

Gingerly, they made their way across the slide, above the sharp drop, and down on the other side to the shoreline. They headed on for the beach that Alan had described, and came to a bend in the river. The beach was around the other side. But now there was no shoreline. It had been washed away, and the bank rose vertically at least 100 feet.

Spring floodwaters had left only a scattering of rocks and boulders next to the high vertical bank.

Getting to the beach wasn't going to be quite as easy as Alan thought. He was a bit embarrassed and, truth be known, was too stubborn to turn back. He was encouraged by recollections that from the elusive beach a gradual slope led up to the upper trail. From there, they'd have an easy walk back to their car.

Undaunted, the intrepid hikers... often balancing precariously on slippery and unstable boulders... jumped from rock to rock. They edged their way around the vertical rock outcropping. Occasionally, a loose rock gave way. A foot here and there went under water.

Finally, they made it to the beach... or, what was left, as it turned out.

They reached a huge flat rock and rested. There, they were treated to a spectacular view downstream of the turbulent river roiling through a narrow gorge. Great view, but no beach... it was gone, too. And they wouldn't be able to go further downstream, even if they wanted to. At that point, the rock walls of the gorge rose straight up at least 75 feet on both sides.

They climbed onto a flat rock sticking out of the steep cliff for a rest. Alan looked around for the trail he remembered... the one heading up a gently sloping valley from the beach. It was gone. All that Alan could see was a steep bank where the valley had been. Spring runoff had swept it away.

They agreed neither had any interest in climbing this 150-foot cliff of dirt, sand and loose rock.

Moments earlier turning back had not even been a consideration. Now, it was their best alternative. Worse yet, shadows were beginning to shroud the deep valley. Mid-day had turned into late afternoon.

It was tricky navigating back upstream along the shoreline. Loose rocks again threatened ankles. Their footwear was soaked again. He wore hiking boots. Being a warm day, Sherry had chosen sturdy hiking sandals. She'd been confident the prominent grips made them suitable for their plans. They were, until then.

As they made their way back upstream, they kept looking for signs of that 'lower trail'. Nothing. An hour later, still no sign of it. They rounded a bend and to their surprise, there was the falls. High above them they saw the railings of the visitor lookout they'd left earlier in the day. They'd walked all the way back along the shore. There was no trail up to the lookout anymore. Nothing. Just sheer rock.

“Oh shit!” Alan said, realizing every single trail had been washed out. Spring run-off had been unusually aggressive that year.

They began to retrace their steps, looking for a means of ascent. Sherry’s sandals were making ‘squish, squish’ sounds as they went.

Finally, they came to a narrow stretch of riverbank that seemed less steep than elsewhere. That stretch of dirt and sand and rock reached upward to bushes and trees. It seemed shorter than the rest, maybe 100 feet. They decided to try. They’d need to angle back and forth switchback style, up to the nearest clump of shrubs.

Alan wished he’d brought that rope he’d left in the car... he was sure they wouldn’t need it. Usually didn’t. Sherry wished they’d never tried this hike... she resolved to wear hiking boots, next time. And would.

Sherry went first.

It took just three or four steps. Her sandals quickly filled with dirt and sand. The other bad news was the sandals had stored large quantities of water. The dirt turned into slippery mud, causing her feet to slip around. The oozing water eventually washed away the mud, leaving sharp sand and pebbles that felt to the bottoms of her feet the size of boulders.

Now, it’s one thing to navigate a steep cliff. It’s quite another when the cliff is composed of unstable dirt, sand and gravel... and big loose rocks much larger than anyone should ever consider standing under.

Sherry began to find truth in the saying ‘two steps forward, one step back’, as did Alan who was close behind. After much struggling, they sat to rest. The roots of an aspen tree above them were tantalizingly close now, laid bare by spring runoff.

They headed up... again. Their goal: those roots. Sherry went first. Alan was close behind.

In a few minutes, she was almost within reach of one large root... just a few more steps. She reached up. Her feet slid back. Again, she climbed up, and again her feet slid half way back. She reached for the roots again. No luck.

Sherry looked down at Alan; she was obviously frustrated and becoming tired. Alan could see it on her face.

She looked back up, and set out again, determined.

Alan looked up. There, above him, was a shapely and attractive and very feminine derriere.

Hmmm, he thought. *Dare I?*

They hadn't known each other all that long.

He feared the action he was considering might involve a lot more intimacy than he should presume to take... perhaps too much for newly-mets.

Sherry's feet slipped back. Up went his hand.

Hmm, he thought again. *Nice bum!*

The boost was just enough for Sherry to grab the root and pull herself up behind the tree. Alan scrambled up beside her.

They looked at each other. They smiled knowingly about their first intimacy. And then Sherry and Alan made their way back to the falls and the parking lot.

On the drive back to town, both burst into laughter.

Dressing Chickens

(Warning: This story contains descriptions that may be disturbing to some. However, for those raised on farms... no surprises and a touch of humor.)

She stood there as if frozen, her back pressed to the fence. Then she screamed; it was a piercing scream of terror. A headless chicken was staggering toward her, its wings flapping, legs churning... blood spurting from its severed neck.

I confess. It was thoughtless of me, upsetting my city-raised wife like that.

No excuses, but as a kid raised on a family farm I'd learned from early childhood about growing and raising our own food. We didn't think twice about what had to be done. We just did it—weeding the garden, milking cows, slopping the pigs, dressing chickens.

But Judi was a city-raised girl.

At this point, I'm going to drag my friend Mike into this. He became an innocent accomplice in the distress I caused my good wife. Mike and I go back a long way. He and I were the entire first grade class in our one-room country school. Over time, our lives took us in different directions but Mike and I would reconnect every so often. We are privileged to have one of those rare and rewarding friendships.

One reconnection occurred while I was attending university. My wife and I were married, with two kids at the time. Mike and his family were operating his family farm 60 miles away from the university town.

It was just after Christmas and Mike had invited us to visit. The two families were meeting for the first time. Our wives and children hit it off immediately. Our kids were of similar ages. Over the next months, our visits became frequent.

It was during one visit early in the new year that Mike made a proposition: would we go half and half on a yearling steer, on a pig and on 50 chickens? Being a university student had put our family on a tight budget. This offer would save us hundreds of dollars in grocery bills. We jumped at the chance.

The deal was, Mike's family would arrange for the steer, the pig and the newly hatched chicks. We would pay for the feed and they would provide the housing and care. The two families would share other costs. I still think he got the short end of the stick, but he insisted. He always was a good guy.

That was the attractive side of the deal. It was consummating the other side that caused all the grief.

To save money the two families would take a weekend in the fall to 'dress' the mature chickens and get them ready for the freezer. A professional butcher would prepare the steer and the pig, at a shared cost.

And so it came to pass, we arrived on the agreed weekend in the fall to visit and to complete the final part of the bargain – dressing the chickens.

Mike's effervescent wife Carol had got up early the morning after our arrival. She came in for breakfast just as the rest of us were waking. She'd been out to build a fire under a large iron caldron about three feet high and two feet in diameter, filled with water.

"The water'll be hot by the time we need it," Carol said. We all understood what she meant. That is, all except Judi as it turned out.

We'd been advised to bring rubber boots. That made sense; we'd be working in the chicken run. Cleaning chicken droppings and other things from shoes is not a pleasant experience.

With breakfast over and everyone appropriately attired in old clothes and rubber boots the four of us headed for the chicken run. Mike said we had 34 chickens to dress.

That meant 17 for each family, an impressive amount to our family. The rest of the 50 we'd bought hadn't made it through the summer. Fatality rates are high among newly hatched chicks.

The water in the reservoir was hot and steaming in the cool morning air of early fall. Carol demonstrated by sticking a couple of fingers in and then withdrawing them rapidly, with a grimace.

Two big chopping blocks were positioned in the center of the chicken run. They'd obviously been cut from large trees and saved. The rest of those trees probably had become firewood, perhaps some even used to heat the water.

"Here," Mike said, handing me a large machete with an 18-inch blade. "I sharpened these the other day, one for you and one for me." He held his up. "We're all set." To illustrate, he swung his machete down into the three-foot high chopping block. The blade sank easily into the end-grain wood.

"You probably remember," Mike said with his beaming trademark smile. (I'd grown up on a farm two miles away.) "You need to sneak up on them from behind."

I nodded.

My wife was in the chicken run watching us begin to stalk the chickens. To some people, chickens may seem not all that smart, but evidently they sense when someone or something is after them. My wife enjoyed immensely watching us run around trying to catch the elusive birds.

The trick, I recalled, was to catch the chickens from behind by their legs. That way they could be upended and taken to the chopping block where their head and neck could be extended more easily, and then the deed done.

It became a contest between Mike and I – which of us would catch a chicken first and lop off its head. Turns out we both got chickens to the chopping block almost at the same time. Okay, okay, Mike was a lot faster.

By now, my wife was finding all this immensely hilarious. She had a bubbly personality, and laughed easily and loud; she was famous for having a delightful laugh that could be heard miles away.

Mike and I looked at each other. We swung our machetes. Off came the heads. We dropped the headless birds on the ground, and turned to catch the next ones. This was normal procedure. Headless chickens scamper around, blood spurting briefly. It's a good thing for the meat, but to the unfamiliar it can seem quite gory. Suddenly I heard a horrendous frightened scream. It was Judi. I whirled around, fearing she had been hurt. Judi had been standing next to the hot water reservoir.

There she was, hands stretched out in front of her, trying to run backwards toward the fence, stumbling, struggling to keep from falling in the poop-littered chicken run. All the while, she kept staring down in fear at a headless chicken flopping towards her a few feet away.

That's when I finally remembered that Judi had been raised in town. I should have realized this sooner. She'd never experienced this before, the process of 'dressing chickens'. When we'd talked about it earlier I'd made passing references and made assumptions – and had not explained precisely what that meant.

Make no mistake; Judi had more poise and courage than almost anyone you're ever likely to meet. And we're not sure exactly how she disappeared from the chicken run, but she was gone in a flash. Carol found her in the farmhouse. By then she was composed but adamantly refusing to go anywhere near the chicken run. She insisted on finding some other way to do her part, and she did, pulling pinfeathers.

Mike and I finished our jobs with the machetes. Carol and the two of us dunked the carcasses in the scalding water to loosen the feathers. The three of us plucked the chickens and removed the innards. And a now perfectly calm Judi, firmly ensconced in the house, pulled the pinfeathers from most of the 34 chickens that we 'dressed' that day.

The Halloween Outhouse Caper

The family men in our remote farm community hated Halloween. That was the time of year when local teenagers would sneak out at night and topple neighborhood outhouses. They thought it was funny. But pranks like that meant we had to wait, sometimes under great pressure you understand, for our fathers to set the outhouses upright again.

It's not that the outhouses were damaged. Most were built so well they were darned near indestructible. However, they did not function as planned while lying on their backs.

No one in our area at the time had indoor toilets or septic systems. So, huge importance was given to these vital outdoor plumbing facilities, usually found a distance downwind from the farm homes. And thus, much urgency was attached to the early resurrection of them the morning after Halloween. After all, certain calls of nature demanded prompt attention. And one should not ignore that other hazard of toppled toilets – the highly odiferous pit left unprotected adjacent to the prone outhouse.

So how could this Halloween vandalism... those vexing pranks... be stopped? The community was perplexed. Winter passed, spring and summer came and went, but no agreed-upon solution had emerged. Then, the harvesting once again was done and the fall season for social events got underway. Halloween was approaching.

One day, neighbors gathered for a thorough airing of the issues, so to speak. The meeting followed a year of discussions at community picnics, dances, box socials, weddings, funerals and other pretexts for gatherings, mostly at the local one-room country school. A number of solutions had been advanced. These included guard dogs and shotguns with shells filled with rock salt. Mercifully, none of these more aggressive notions got much support beyond wishful thinking among our fathers. The matter remained unresolved.

Then came the fall dinner and dance. During the meal, one of the quieter farmers took advantage of a lull in the growing ambient noise to speak up:

"I've an idea," Henry said. "Why not just move our outhouses?"

"What!" another farmer came thundering into the conversation before Henry could continue, his mouth propelled by homemade moonshine. "Are you kidding me? What're ya saying... load our outhouses on flatbeds and tow them away? Y'all gotta be kiddin' me! Ha, ha, ha! That don't make no sense at all! What'll we use in the meantime?"

"We might as well tie them down," laughed another man. "That's a dumb idea!"

Henry sat quietly through the criticism and heckling.

Then, during another lull, Henry added calmly: "Just move them off the hole a bit. Move them backward... you know, behind the pit. That'll fix 'em."

Quiet descended. The doubters began to listen. Maybe this guy wasn't full of *it* after all.

"Those kids... when they tip our outhouses over, they always push them from the front. Right? They tip them over backward. We just need to hide the hole with some tree branches."

Henry's idea became a hit. The neighborhood buzzed with excitement as Halloween approached. Apprehension and annoyance was transformed into anticipation. Neighbors teamed up to help move each other's outhouse surreptitiously after dark on the fateful night.

The men had overlooked one small detail:

The culprits were almost certainly teenaged boys from the area. They would belong to the very families supposedly conspiring against them. The boys couldn't help but be tipped off about the traps being set for them.

Ah, but the boys had also overlooked something.

They underestimated Henry. He didn't tell the others about Part Two of his plan. Henry had guessed who were the most likely suspects, and had assumed correctly they would learn about the traps being planned for them. He began quietly putting into effect Part Two.

To do so, Henry went down the road to see Pete, his neighbor half a mile away. Neither had teenaged boys. Pete agreed to Henry's secret Part Two, and agreed to keep it just between them.

The plan was to outsmart the Halloween pranksters by moving their outhouses in the opposite direction to the public plan, that is, forward, not backward. This would leave the pits wide open behind the outhouses, and that's where the teenage pranksters would think it was safe to execute their nefarious deeds.

After dark on Halloween night, Henry and Pete helped each move their outhouses forward. Earlier, they'd cut tree branches and bushes. They used these to camouflage the unprotected pits. Then, dressed in dark clothes, each sat in the shadows beside their respective back porches waiting to observe as the anticipated events unfolded.

The next morning, Henry and Pete exchanged stories over coffee, unable to suppress their hilarity. Between outbursts of laughter they described for each other, which neighbor's boy had gone how deep into the obnoxious substances at the bottom of those outhouse pits... along with the surprisingly coarse words the boys had used to express their dismay, and how quickly each culprit had run to nearby ponds or water troughs and jumped in fully clothed.

From that day forward, nary an outhouse for miles around ever tumbled again, except perhaps of its own accord... from old age, after many years of faithful service, relieving its owners of their burdens. Naturally.

The Foot Race

John Thomas Shelley was a big man, both in stature and in his line of work. He was tall and sported an abundant girth that strained the captain's chair where he presided over a family table seating up to 12.

JT could be firm. He needed to be. He'd fathered 10 children and was a leader in a dangerous job. But he also had a well-developed sense of humor. Those attributes probably helped him and his kindly wife survive raising their nine rambunctious boys, and a daughter who JT joked half seriously was the only sensible one among their offspring. Somehow, he also found time to be a firefighter, which culminated in a career-capping five-year appointment as chief of the city's fire department.

Even before Chief Shelley retired at age 65, his children and grandchildren were teasing him about his girth – chiding him that his belly was probably as big around as he was tall. Not surprising then, he'd be the last person you'd expect to engage in a foot race. But he did.

Soon after retiring, JT and his warm-hearted spouse, Ellen, decided on a road trip. Their children were grown. Most of them and the grandchildren lived close to home. But a few had gravitated to other locations. They missed seeing these family members, so the newly retired couple set off to visit them.

First stop was a farm owned by their daughter, Pearl and her husband, John. The couple had three children at the time, ranging in age from six to 11. JT was fond of calling them scallywags, a term of endearment he'd applied to his own offspring.

When JT and Ellen arrived for their visit, the adults engaged in their usual enthusiastic hugs and kisses. The children found these seemingly excessive shows of affection quite underwhelming, in their words, 'yucky'. And that's what led to the challenge.

"Grandpa?" Carol asked. "Is your belt really as far around as you are tall?"

"Carol!" Pearl admonished her eldest child, embarrassed. "Don't talk to your grandfather like that."

"Sorry, Dad," Pearl said, glancing sheepishly toward her father.

"Oh, that's all right, dear," replied JT, releasing one of his trademark belly laughs. "They're just being kids. Remember when you were that age?"

"But I heard what Uncle Roy said," Carol persisted. "He said Grandpa's stomach is such a long way around that his belt is longer than he is high."

Carol's younger brother Jim joined the merriment. Their uncle Roy, who was accompanying his parents on their trip, looked away, pretending to be preoccupied in something else.

"Yeah," Jim chuckled. "Grandpa sure does have a big belly!"

"Shush you two," Pearl said sharply, growing annoyed. (She called it, 'becoming cross'.) "You mustn't say things like that!"

"It's okay," JT repeated, eying his only daughter with a sly smile. "Do you mind if I handle this?"

"Sure, Dad," Pearl replied, relieved and curious. She'd learned while growing up her father could be a stern disciplinarian, but he also had a sly and mischievous sense of humor.

JT turned his attention to Carol and Jim.

"Okay, you two scallywags," he said, smiling. "Get over here."

The two youngsters inched forward, quiet and nervous, uncertain what their grandfather wanted.

"I'm going to make a bet with you two," he said in his most commanding fire chief tone.

"What kind of bet, Grandpa?" Carol said timidly, glancing quickly at her brother. Both wondered apprehensively what their grandfather was up to.

"You think I'm fat, don't you?" he said rhetorically. Not waiting for them to answer he added: "Well, I'll just bet I can outrun the both of you! Do you want to take me up on that?"

"YEAH, Grandpa!" Carol cried out. She was never shy about a challenge, especially one she felt absolutely certain of winning. Carol had become known in their area for her athletic talents. She'd won several races at their school's field days.

Carol and Jim exchanged a look of understanding. They quietly took into account Grandpa's abundant girth. Both were convinced that if his advanced age didn't take him out of contention, the size of his belly would most certainly do so.

Full disclosure here: JT was a big man, to be sure. And while his girth was substantial, the truth is that it was not all that much larger than the middle age spreads common among men his age. But to a couple of pre-teens with delusions of glory, his abundant belly seemed huge, offering the promise of a decidedly favorable advantage.

The challenge was set! The three lined up in the back yard.

Then, Grandpa raised his left hand in a gesture of command, calling for a pause.

He walked over to his petite wife and removed his navy blue suit coat. He folded it carefully and laid it on Ellen's outstretched arms. Grinning over at Carol and Jim, he undid the buttons of his matching vest, folded it and draped it over his coat. Next he removed the clip holding his tie to his shirt and clipped it onto his maroon and black diagonal striped tie, which he removed and folded with care. He winked slyly at Ellen. A broad smile appeared on his face as he removed his fedora hat and placed it on top of the pile of clothing in his wife's arms. Finally, he unbuttoned the sleeves of his starched white shirt and rolled up the cuffs. He was ready.

"You guys ready?" he asked, as if he'd been waiting for them all along.

"Yes, Grandpa," Carol replied. There was a hint of impatience.

"Well then, what are we waiting for?" he chided them.

The three lined up in the back yard. The finish line would be a dirt path about 50 feet away. The well-traveled route, worn through the grass of the sparse lawn, connected the back door of the farm home on their left with the family outhouse, tucked discretely behind the garage on the right.

"You tell us when to 'go'," Grandpa said, turning to Betty Ann, the youngest of the three children, standing on the sidelines. Too little to be a serious contender, she was brimming with pride at being named the designated starter.

Betty Ann could barely wait for the three racers to check each other carefully to ensure their opponents were lined up fairly.

"Ready, Go!" Betty Ann cried gleefully. She forgot to say 'Set', an oversight that would create much controversy later at supper.

Carol and Jim sprinted off immediately. They opened an early lead over Grandpa and quickly expanded it. Soon, Carol was ahead of Jim by more than two yards. Jim was running hard, managing to stay a couple of steps ahead of Grandpa.

Grandma Ellen cheered Grandpa. Pearl and John cheered their children. Betty Ann wasn't sure whom to support, so she cheered for everyone.

As they reached the halfway point, Carol had expanded her lead even more. She looked like a winner for sure. Her face glowed with confidence.

By now Jim was struggling, his lead over Grandpa rapidly dwindling. He wasn't known as a strong runner.

Then to everyone's surprise except his, Grandpa

turned on the speed. First he overtook Jim handily. The race was quickly approaching the finish line... Grandpa was still several yards behind the happily smiling leader.

Carol heard the rapid fall of her grandfather's footsteps behind her. She urged herself on harder, nearing the limit of her considerable speed.

They were just a few yards from the finish line when Carol took a quick look over her shoulder. A mistake. Her glance back threw her off course, slowing her ever so slightly. It was just enough for Grandpa to pass her, mere inches from the finish line.

The race was over. By some miracle, Grandpa had won! Carol and Jim were dumbfounded, and feeling decidedly contrite.

There was Grandpa, just beyond the dirt path finish line, bent over, hands on his knees, breathing heavily, beads of sweat on a bald head encircled by a fringe of white hair. He glanced up, smiled paternally at his two young scallywags, and said not a word.

Ellen and John applauded and cheered Grandpa. Pearl hurried over to comfort the defeated twosome, smiling understandingly. Betty Ann applauded everyone.

At supper that evening, Grandpa remained stoic in his victory while around him everyone engaged in chatter about the race, the closeness of the contest or lack thereof, the merits of the officiating, i.e., the legality of the starter's oversight, and the suitability of the finish line.

Through it all, Grandpa would glance from time to time, first at Carol and then at Jim, and smile contentedly each time to himself and them. And each time that he did so, Ellen would poke her tiny sharp elbow into an especially tender spot in his ribs only she know about.

Nothing more was said about Grandpa's belly, for a while that is.

We're not sure who did it or exactly when, but some time later an anonymous scallywag came up with the phrase, 'Shelley Belly'. It stuck. No one's fessed up.

The Anniversary

Art and Sally planned a very special celebration for their 25th wedding anniversary. It turned out even better.

The couple was to meet in Frankfurt, and wander through Europe for two weeks on a second honeymoon. The plan was no plan: no agenda, no deadlines, no reservations. Just spontaneous wandering... and all quite romantic.

Sally would arrive from Norway, where she'd been a delegate to the World YWCA Congress, and Art would fly in from their home in Canada. His flight landed at mid-day; Sally's was due just before suppertime.

Perfect timing! Art thought. *We'll have a nice dinner and get to bed early.*

They'd been apart for 10 days... the couple had some loving to catch up on.

Art phoned to reserve a quiet table in the hotel's classy Bavarian-style restaurant. Then, he finished writing the special anniversary card for Sally he'd brought from home. He propped it up on the antique wood table in their hotel room.

Art was watching the news on TV when Sally phoned from the lobby.

"We'll be right up," she said.

He was excited, and then realized Sally had said, 'We'.

We? He thought. *Must be someone traveling with her stopping over on their way home from the conference.*

After 25 years, Art had learned not to be surprised. Sally would often 'pick up strays'. Helping others was imbedded deeply within her nature. He resigned himself to enduring an exchange of polite greetings before getting on with their own intimate reunion and private anniversary celebrations.

When the knock came, Art leaped up eagerly to

answer the door. Sally was not alone. Standing in the hallway beside her was a large mature woman Art recognized. She was ignored momentarily while Sally and Art exchanged affectionate hugs and passionate kisses.

Finally, Art said, "Hi Jenny." They shared friendly hugs. "Good to see you again."

"Nice room," Sally said, stepping through the doorway. Her comment was typically generous. Floor space not occupied by the queen-sized bed, table and two chairs was about the size of an old-fashioned walk-in phone booth. It was sumptuous, but tiny.

"Jenny's booked into a room down the hall," Sally said. "She's going to join us for supper. I knew you wouldn't mind."

Oh shit! Art thought. *So much for our romantic dinner.*

His dismay was about to increase.

Jenny departed for her room, leaving Art and Sally to enjoy their reunion in the few minutes before dinner.

The anniversary couple discussed their travel plans. They were to head south on Germany's famous Autobahn the next morning and start their second honeymoon with a circle tour of Switzerland. Art said he'd not been able to upgrade their tiny rented car as hoped. They would be stuck with the Kadet they'd booked months earlier. The two-door vehicle had the appearance of a runt cousin to a Volkswagen beetle, but smaller inside.

"It could get a bit tight," Sally ventured.

"Yes," Art said with resignation. He was relieved Sally's traveling wardrobe was like her: small, compact and thoroughly unpretentious. A few pairs of shorts and jeans, an assortment of t-shirts and sweatshirts, a nightie or two, some flip-flops and lots of clean underwear was all neatly enclosed in a small suitcase.

"I guess we'll have to squeeze our suitcases into the back seat beside Jenny," Sally said as if thinking out loud.

"WHAT?" Art replied, struck by a flash of disbelief. He was at once thunderstruck, not surprised and secretly proud of his tiny caring wife of a quarter century... but he had to admit he was mostly dismayed.

After years of many such experiences, he was overtaken by a vivid premonition of what he would hear next. It came, all right, and he resigned himself to it.

"I invited Jenny to come along," Sally confessed, a twinkle in her green hazel eyes. "I knew you wouldn't mind."

The hell I wouldn't, Art was thinking. He knew better than to say so. Instead, he replied:

"But, Honey, this is our second honeymoon! We planned it. Just for the two of us."

"I know, Honey," Sally replied. (They both called each other 'Honey'. It confused the hell out of strangers!)

"But when I was telling Jenny about our plans, she said to me, 'I sure would like to visit Europe some day, too, but I don't have anyone to share it with... I won't go alone.'

"Well, you know, I just couldn't go without her. I was sure you'd understand."

Awe, shit! Art thought. The only saving grace was that their traveling companion was the living legend known as Jenny MacLeod. Sally had spoken often about this woman's amazing personality and remarkable accomplishments. Art had met her briefly a few times. He admired her achievements and had wanted to get to know her a little better. This wasn't what he had in mind.

Jenny MacLeod was a single mother who'd performed miracles as head of a YWCA women's residence in a remote mining town. The residence had been borderline bankrupt and derelict when she took over managing the place. After becoming executive director, Jenny moved with her two daughters into a tiny one-bedroom apartment in the residence. Within five years, the residence was in good repair, freshly painted inside and out, debt free and making a profit. And in the decades since, it had generated an impressive profit every year. The achievement had made her a 'poster girl' in the YWCA movement.

Art spent a restless night worrying about how to accommodate three adults and their luggage in that wheeled sardine can they'd reserved.

The trio arrived at the airport car rental office at mid-morning. That was shamefully late by the demanding standards that most Germans lived by.

Art felt a sense of foreboding as he handed the car rental agent their confirmation. The agent took his time reading the document, phoning twice in the process. Art's anxiety soared.

"I'm very sorry, sir," the agent said in lightly accented English. "We are all out of Kadets. The last one was rented less than an hour ago. According to your confirmation, you were supposed to pick your car up at 9 a.m. It's past 10 o'clock now. Can we arrange a substitute for you?"

Oh, sure, Art thought. *That damned Kadet was just a come-on. I should have guessed it was a scam. Shit! Those assholes!'*

"Yeah, sure," Art replied. "What have you got left and how much is it? We need a car for two weeks. What kind of a deal can you give us?"

"Well sir," the agent replied with a knowing grin. "We have available for you and your ladies a full size Audi sedan. A very nice car, sir... top of the Audi line. It's really a luxury car, sir."

Just as I thought,' Art told himself. *The ol' bait-and-switch.*

"So," Art inquired. "How much is this one? And what else do you have available?"

"Well, sir," the agent replied. "This is the very best

we can do for you, I'm afraid. Like I said, sir, it's a very nice car."

"Alright," said Art impatiently. "How much?"

"Well, sir," the agent replied firmly. "Since we didn't have the car you ordered available, the rate will be the same as for the Kadet."

Through his astonishment, Art was barely aware of the agent showing him where to sign and asking for his credit card.

Every piece of their luggage fit nicely into the trunk of the large Audi V-8 sedan. Jenny would have the back seat all to herself.

As they set off south on the Autobahn, Art's thoughts bounced between their great good vehicular fortune and getting used to the fact his wife of 25 years had invited someone to ride shotgun on their second honeymoon. *Better get over it,* he instructed himself firmly.

Jenny turned out to be a surprising asset during their tour and, in time, Art came to admit, a welcome traveling companion. She was intelligent and nimbly astute, knowing just when to disappear during intimate moments.

With one exception.

They had ventured into France near Strasbourg, planning to stay the night in some small historic rural town. During their tour, they had made it a practice to not decide beforehand where they'd go the next day, so reservations were never made. They'd been doing this successfully for days. France turned out to be quite different. First, the trio didn't know that a huge region-wide medieval festival was underway in that part of the country. That day, they'd traveled long and it was late afternoon as they went town-to-town-to-town looking for a place to stay. Everything was booked. As the hours passed and the 'no vacancies' continued, their preferred standards for accommodation dipped lower and lower.

By then, despite Sally's characteristic Pollyanna

façade, Jenny's reserve was eroding. She had begun responding to Art's mounting irritation by suggesting to Sally the two women needed 'to feed the monkey'... meaning Art. That humor served to break the tension.

It was getting dark as they pulled up before a nondescript 'pension' (a.k.a., bed and breakfast). There was enough light to see the 'no vacancy' sign and a tiny elderly lady standing guard on the front steps beside the sign.

Irrepressible Sally somehow managed to summon the energy to turn on the charm... in English.

The old woman was unimpressed... and kept shaking her head vigorously, 'no'.

No vacancy and no interest in the trio's plight.

Sally reverted to her sketchy recollections of high school French and put an after-burner under her charm.

The ancient lady stood.

That's a good sign, Art thought. Jenny verbalized the sentiment.

The old woman shrugged her shoulders and turned.

Sally's face lit up as she motioned to the others.

They followed the old woman around to the back of the unkept building and through a door. Up they went, two flights of stairs. A door took them unexpectedly outside and up a rickety flight of stairs to door into a third floor. It opened into a long storage area, beneath unfinished rafters. It was maybe 40 or 50 feet long. At both ends, the gables were filled with stacks of wooden boxes and ancient furniture.

Bed sheets hung from horizontal braces between the rough-hewn 4×6 inch rafters. They formed a makeshift hallway. The old woman lifted one sheet. There squatted a lumpy double bed. At one end of the enclosure, near the middle of the attic, was another pile of wood boxes, stacked to the rafters. On the other side was another double bed, lumpy and sagging like the other. It would be an exaggeration to describe either as a bedroom.

Pensions provide only breakfast. The hungry trio ventured forth from their garret, as they affectionately called it, and found their supper nearby at a dark and noisy establishment in the form of beer and bar food.

The next morning, Jenny departed again from her characteristic reserve, describing some nocturnal squeaking and squawking that woke her... and that she insisted came from Art and Sally's enclosure. The couple declined ownership.

Jenny had other surprises. Early in their tour, she'd offered to handle the couple's newly purchased video camera. Although tech-challenged, Jenny soon mastered the red on-off switch and marveled at the magic of the zoom lens. But she never quite understood the camera was recording voice along with the video – much to her later embarrassment. As she commented later, "never say in private what you don't want heard in public".

Shortly after the trio arrived back home, Jenny asked to borrow the videocassettes of their tour. Art and Sally obliged – they hadn't found time to edit the 20+ hours of video, mostly recorded by Jenny. They assumed Jenny wanted to get the cassettes copied. Two months later, their cassettes arrived back, along with a professionally edited 60-minute video of the key highlights of their trip as well as a brilliantly written script/photo album. It was a welcome and gracious 'thank you' that made sharing the trip with Jenny more than worthwhile.

A Hitch at Hatchet Lake

Hatchet Lake is frozen most of the year. A fly-in fishing camp there opens in early June. It closes when the sub-Arctic lake begins to freeze over again in September. Going fishing on the lake too early is risky, even for those well accustomed to Mother Nature's unpredictable temperament.

Henry and Andrew were among a dozen men who flew to Hatchet Lake Lodge early one season. It was mid-June. From windows in the float-equipped plane, Henry saw patches of open water along the shoreline and a bay where the plane would land. The summer season for this wilderness lodge was about to begin.

The two men were among the leadership of a company who'd flown there for three days of 'get-away' planning meetings and recreation. A day of fishing on this trophy lake was scheduled prior to their departure.

Work done, the group woke to their day of fishing. Two people were assigned to each boat. First Nations guides supplied by the lodge handled the 20-foot aluminum boats. Henry and Andrew were paired up. Back home, they had adjoining offices and got along well. They were looking forward to fishing together.

The fishing pairs set off in different directions, local guides at the helm. This was an ideal lake for those devoted to fishing. The ice cold water would ensure the flesh of the fish was firm and flavorful especially that early in the season.

At noon, the teams met as arranged for a 'shore lunch' on a tree-covered island. Fish caught that morning were pooled and prepared for lunch. The visitors had never witnessed such a lunch, nor the main cooking implement used. It was four feet in diameter, shaped like a deep gold pan and was placed on a roaring campfire. At least a dozen one-pound bricks of lard were tossed in. When the melted lard became bubbling hot grease, two-inch cubes of Whitefish and Northern Pike were thrown in to cook. One bite and those assembled quickly lined up for seconds.

Fishing that afternoon would be a competition. The boat with the most fish caught would win both a suitably gaudy trophy and, more important, bragging rights. Off the teams went, in all different directions, in 'hot' pursuit of glory. Temperatures were just above freezing.

The guide in Henry and Andrew's boat, a confident twinkle in his eye, pointed off into the distance across the lake to the other side of a peninsula. The guide's English was marginal; his two passengers presumed he was pointing to a bay beyond the point of land. Off they went.

Andrew and Henry were huddled over, one on the middle seat, the other in the bow, their backs to the bitterly cold wind blowing off the lake. They were facing back toward the guide, as he sped the boat across the wide lake toward the large bay. Soon, the nearest land was at least a mile away.

Suddenly the guide cut the engine. The sounds he made had the unmistakable tones of a heart-felt curse. He shook his head, and pointed forward.

Henry and Andrew poked their heads out from within their parka hoods. They looked around. Their boat was surrounded by ice. The two found it hard to believe; the last they'd looked the boat was in open water. The guide eventually was able to explain the wind had come up strongly and quickly, and changed direction unexpectedly. It had blown 'pack ice' across their path and behind them.

They were trapped!

Andrew looked at the ice. It seemed 'rotten', that is, it appeared broken into small pieces. Using gestures and sounds, he managed to ask the guide why not run the boat up onto the ice and then push it to an open stretch of water 20 yards or so away? Andrew reasoned there were three of them and the boat was aluminum, so it was light.

The guide shook his head. He pointed to the ice. Andrew reached over the gunwales with a paddle and poked the ice. It was loose. He could hear a pleasant light tinkling sound coming from it. He reached over and grabbed a chunk. It was round, irregular, and about the diameter of a water tumbler. He lifted it. It kept coming and coming. Finally, Henry and he were pulling. What came into the boat was a shard of ice more than three feet long. The light tinkling sound they were hearing was coming from millions of shards of ice gently bouncing off each other like wind chimes. Only a few inches of ice was poking above the water. Most was below, like millions of tall skinny icebergs. All of the ice as far as they could see was the same, the guide assured them, using of bits of English, and his mother tongue but mostly gestures.

The point was the ice could not be walked on, boated on or pushed through. And it was starting to get dusk.

Henry and Andrew looked at each other, and started laughing. Between them, they'd caught just one eight-pound Northern Pike that day. They talked about what that fish would taste like raw, eaten in the boat as they waited overnight, possibly longer, to reach land.

Andrew asked the guide, "Lodge?"

The guide understood the word and gestured with his right thumb over his shoulder. They were headed in the wrong direction!

No matter, Henry and Andrew finally realized. The boat couldn't be turned around anyway; it was caught fast in the pack ice. And starting the motor would draw ice into the propeller, damaging it.

Both looked to the guide for... uh... guidance. The guide sat there looking calm, scanning the sky, his dark eyes squinting almost closed.

Henry and Andrew finally managed to ask the guide whether they might be forced to stay overnight. The guide just shrugged. Then, attempting to be helpful, he gestured to an island, implying they might possibly drift over close to it before nightfall. Andrew and Henry didn't receive that as the good news the guide seemed to be making it out to be. They were already cold and the backs of their parkas were wet from spray thrown up earlier by the boat. Neither relished the prospect of spending the night in the boat. And building a campfire and a crude shelter, with no tools, no tarps, no bedding and no cooking supplies would not be much of an improvement.

But they did have the fish. They laughed again, nervously this time.

The daylight faded further. The guide sat at the transom, his face placid and directed forward, past Henry and Andrew. Then he sat up. The fur around the hood of his parka stirred uncertainly. A slight breeze had come up. He gestured behind them.

Henry and Andrew turned around. A path had opened up through the pack ice at the front of the boat. It was about five feet wide and zigzagged off into the distance. Other pathways seemed to meet it from time to time. Some of them reached open water near the shore of the mainland.

The guide started the motor. He gently turned the throttle, moving the boat forward slowly, concentrating hard to avoid getting ice in the propeller. Finally, the boat reached open water.

The guide stopped the boat and idled the motor. He managed to explain that a breeze had come up from the right direction. It had shifted a lake full of ice. Huge! In the process, pathways had opened in the pack ice, allowing them to reach shore. He didn't explain what might have happened had the breeze come from the wrong direction. Andrew and Henry didn't ask.

When they reached the lodge, the guide became the happy owner of the eight-pound Northern Pike. Henry and

Andrew didn’t win the fishing contest. But they did earn some story-telling rights.

First Seniors Discount

Rights of passage have their moments. Some are memorable... some are humorous. Theirs was both.

Once upon a time in cottage country lived a petite little woman named Janet. She was married to a man eight years older who adored her. Both loved golf. They'd retired early to a cottage near a few golf courses. From there they could golf in spring, summer and fall, and head south for the winter – to golf some more.

But not everything was all sunlight and roses. As their family had grown up and left home, Janet had begun to sense the approach of a terrible thing... aging. To be clear, she was fearless in almost every way, with one notable exception... that biggie for women: *looking old.* This explained why she had a fitness background, ate carefully, colored her hair, and began spending more and more time with the miracles of modern makeup. (She really hated it when her husband George referred to her make-up bag as her 'Magic Kit'.)

One day, Janet and George decided to try some new golf courses. They sat down and planned an itinerary of interesting courses they wanted to try. Janet volunteered to book hotel rooms and tee times along their route.

The first course offered a seniors discount on green fees for guest players over 60. Janet happily signed George up for the seniors discount – he'd just turned 60 and this would be his first discount. She didn't tell him about the discount, wanting to surprise him.

The couple arrived at the golf course 90 minutes ahead of their 2:43 tee time. They planned to have lunch first. When they finished, Janet volunteered to visit the pro shop and pay their green fees while George settled the lunch bill. That seemed reasonable to George. Janet had something else in mind – she had decided on an impromptu ceremony to present George with the receipt showing his first-ever senior's discount.

A look of ill-concealed outrage was clouding Janet's attractive face when she arrived back at their table. The receipt for the tee times was crumpled tightly in her dainty right fist.

"Do you know what that man back there said to me?" she asked through clenched teeth, gesturing with her right thumb over her shoulder in the general direction of the unfortunate pro shop employee.

Not waiting for a reply, "Do you know what he said?" she repeated, the full fury of bruised dignity gaining momentum.

Surprised by his normally calm wife, George wondered what this was all about. He suspected some exuberant male might have made the mistake of trying to flirt with Janet. She was, after all, quite attractive for a woman approaching – with great reluctance – middle age. The poor unwitting sot would have been in for the shock of his life, George thought, smiling to himself.

Again not waiting for an answer, Janet blurted out: "He asked me if *I* wanted the seniors discount! Can you believe that? He asked *me* if I wanted that damned discount, too!

"The nerve!" Janet continued, her indignity approaching its zenith.

George nodded, but continued to wonder what on Earth his dear wife was going on about... what senior's discount? Regardless, he'd learned long ago to look sympathetic and nod, but to say nothing.

"Do you know what I said to him?" she demanded. Her voice now was half an octave from shrill.

"Uh, no," George managed, hoping the unfortunate anonymous male still had his confidence and his gender attributes in tact.

"I asked him, 'do I *LOOK* like a senior?'" Janet replied, stomping her foot, hand on hips, her anger soaring. "I said to him, 'Just how *old* do you think I am?'"

George knew only too well that no ordinary man could possibly withstand an onslaught of indignation from this petite five-foot-nothing bundle of fearsome kinetic energy. He was convinced the poor guy by now must surely be on his way home with symptoms of Post Traumatic Stress Disorder.

Janet had been a fitness instructor for years. Although eight years younger than George, at 52 she looked closer to 40 and was fiercely proud of it.

"Well, did he apologize?" George ventured cautiously.

"No," Janet replied angrily. "He didn't say a word. The damned nerve!"

That's when Janet realized she'd crushed the milestone receipt in her hand with George's very first senior's discount. She had intended to present it to George with a great flourish. She opened her hand and began sheepishly to smooth the receipt out on the table.

That's when her whole demeanor suddenly changed.

The righteous indignation faded abruptly. It was replaced by a mischievous smile that flashed across her pretty face.

"How about that!" Janet blurted out, chuckling. "Look at this!"

She passed the slip over to George.

The receipt showed charges for two green fees... with two seniors discounts.

All Fired Up

The fire was out of control... the heat so intense the ground was hot, dry and bare on the side of the ridge facing the fire. On the other side, it was bitterly cold. Snow a foot deep covered that slope.

Through the car windshield, the young man could see his friend's body. It was face down, draped over the lip of the huge circular ridge surrounding the raging gas well fire. Brilliant light from the flames outlined his colleague's back and buttocks. His feet and legs were thrust deeply into the snow.

Orville's upper body was toward the screaming inferno. He was lying on his chest, arms bent, his elbows propped up on brittle dead grass, shielding his Speed Graphic press camera. The hood of his parka and jacket were peeled back down past his shoulders. The buttons of his shirt were opened almost to the waist.

Duncan O'Brien felt guilty. Orville had insisted he sit in the car. He'd been there a while. It was the only place to get warm in this vast expanse of treeless rolling prairie.

Suddenly, Duncan saw his colleague trying desperately to block the searing heat bombarding his upper body and head. He watched as Orville raised his parka as a shield. Orville was trying to focus his camera on the blazing natural gas well. It was spewing upward from within a mass of burned and twisted metal lying at the bottom of a bowl-shaped hollow. Fingers of red and blue flames thrust their way through the crumbled remains of the drilling rig and then shot skyward for over 300 feet.

Later, they were told the top half of Orville's body had been exposed to temperatures exceeding 150 degrees Fahrenheit. Yet, he was more than 200 yards from the burning wellhead. The opposite end of his body – his legs and feet – were in temperatures hovering between zero and

10 degrees Fahrenheit. Orville's response was that taken on average he should have been fairly comfortable.

The wild natural gas well resembled a massive screaming blowtorch. It had exploded out of control two days earlier. Orville and Duncan, a young reporter, had been assigned to cover the gas well fire by the daily newspaper where both worked.

Night was fast approaching as Orville finished snapping enough photographs for their first story. Duncan had gathered as many details as he would get that day from a frantic gas well drilling rig supervisor. The two journalists needed to 'file' this developing news story right away. They headed off on the three-hour drive back to the city and the newspaper.

In the newsroom, Duncan and Orville worked late... well into the early morning. Orville prepared a special photo layout for the next day's paper. Duncan wrote a news story to accompany Orville's spectacular photos. In the morning, an editor would send it all to the national news service for transmission to other media across the country and elsewhere.

Their work done, the two hopped into the staff car and headed back out to the burning gas well, taking turns sleeping en route.

For the next few days, the pattern was the same. During the day, they would gather photos and information on the latest developments, and then head back to the newspaper where they prepared updated stories and photo essays, working into the early hours of the following day.

Orville insisted on leaving the office for the trip back at that hour without going home for a few hours sleep. Duncan knew that he feared a senior editor might arrive for work unexpectedly early and insist that a younger photographer handle the rest of the assignment, including photos. Orville wanted none of that. He took his job seriously as photo editor but also relished getting out into the country, camera in hand.

This time, that shared eagerness almost cost them their lives.

Duncan and Orville had become friends well before this assignment. Duncan was green – he had just a few years of experience. But he'd shown an interest in the photo side of journalism and that grabbed Orville's attention. Duncan welcomed Orville's mentorship. Duncan's job frequently took him out into the country. He often needed a photographer. He was delighted when Orville assigned himself to go on as many of these out of town trips as he could.

*

The gas well fire was large and proving to be stubborn. It raged out of control for days. Up close, the roar of the blazing natural gas was so loud firefighters had to communicate with hand signals. It took crews three days just to remove the melted wreckage of the drilling rig and the original wellhead. Another day was needed to prepare for at attempt to re-cap the well, an extremely dangerous job.

The company that owned the well had called in Red Adair, a legendary wild well fighter, to bring the fire under control. As luck would have it, Adair's team had just finished putting out an oil well fire only a few hundred miles away. Many years later, Adair's techniques would be used to extinguish hundreds of oil well fires started by Iraqi dictator Saddam Hussein's army while being chased from Kuwait.

One of Adair's crew explained that to shield their workers from the wellhead heat they'd be working behind a sheet of corrugated metal mounted on a tracked bulldozer. He estimated temperatures were more than 1,000 degrees F at the wellhead.

Duncan and Orville continue making their round trips each day. On site, they parked their car strategically – near enough to the top of the ridge to benefit from the searing heat, but far enough away to avoid being cooked. They lived on junk food, cold strong coffee, and a few shared bottles of whiskey they called personal antifreeze. They napped in the car when they could.

One morning, an Adair firefighter told the two journalists the fiercely burning well would be capped later that day... to standby.

This was it! The moment of excitement... and danger they'd been waiting for. The firefighter explained the work would proceed in stages. First, the firefighters would fill a 45-gallon drum with explosives. Next, the steel drum would be bolted to the end of a 50-foot boom attached to a bulldozer. Firefighters on the crawler tractor would use its big heavy bulldozer blade and sheets of corrugated iron as protection against the heat... and what would follow. The plan was for the operator to guide the boom, positioning the drum over the wellhead... then ignite the explosives.

The theory was the massive explosion would rob the burning natural gas of the oxygen needed for combustion. If that worked, the crew could then begin the hazardous job of placing a new wellhead down through, and over, the screaming rush of raw natural gas, and secure it in place. One spark could spell disaster. If all went well, then a huge valve in the wellhead mechanism could be closed, cutting off the flow of gas.

The procedure was extremely dangerous. First, raw natural gas is deadly... and odorless. The familiar 'rotten egg' odor is added later. Shifting winds could blow the dangerous gas down on unsuspecting firefighters and spectators. Second, the tiniest of sparks could reignite the gas and literally blow up the site again. The explosion would destroy the replacement wellhead equipment, and possibly incinerate some of the firefighters trying to tame the well.

The explosion was enormous... the sound deafening. But it worked! The fire was out. Gingerly, the replacement well head was lowered through the screaming stream of natural gas. No spark. The valve was closed safely. The wild gas was under control.

The news story was over. Bitter cold now descended on the inner side of the bowl-shaped depression around the gas well. A light snow was falling but soon it was staying.

Adair, his crew and employees of the well owner were exhausted but in a celebratory mood as they began preparing to head home.

Duncan and Orville were invited to a tiny village 10 miles away for drinks and a celebration party. The only place to hold it was a distressed old beer hall in what had been a hotel. They went. The place was warm at least.

An hour later, the two journalists could delay their departure no longer. The story was big and needed to be filed. They knew the national news services would be clamoring for their wrap-up story and pictures, and there were no cell links.

It was winter and had grown dark early. Duncan and Orville agreed to take turns driving. Both were exhausted. Duncan agreed to drive first. Orville told this story later:

Sound asleep in the front passenger seat, he was jostled awake when the car took a leap upward and then landed hard. Startled, Orville looked over at the Duncan behind the wheel. The young reporter's eyes were wide open... but he was sound asleep. Orville shook him awake with one hand as the car skidded down a gravel road almost out of control, and with the other hand he struggled to steady the vehicle.

Duncan had indeed fallen asleep. They'd been traveling on a straight paved backcountry road. Sleep took over. Eyes open and sound asleep he'd driven straight across a busy intersecting highway and down onto a secondary gravel road before Orville woke him.

As they stopped to gather themselves, laughing nervously at their close call, a steady stream of transport trucks roared up and down the busy highway behind them.

Orville drove the rest of the way.

Beer Cans and Necklaces

Early in his career, Richard was a concert pianist. He's still in demand. Some venues are a challenge. A recent one turned out to be just that, with a bit of humor thrown in.

Richard and his wife Loydeen were invited to the wedding of a friend's niece. He was also asked to give a concert at the wedding. Richard agreed, with some apprehension. His host assured him they had a piano, but Richard was unsure about the piano's wellbeing.

"Saying we have a piano," Richard said later, "sometimes is akin to being invited to race in the Indy 500 and, after being assured you will have a car, finding out you're driving an old Volkswagen Beetle."

And so it was.

The wedding was a two-day drive. No problem. But Richard guessed – correctly as it turned out – the piano he would be playing was nowhere near his accustomed standards. But then, that would take some doing. You see Richard owns a full-sized grand piano. That's a nine-foot sleek black musical instrument hand made in Germany. It's almost priceless. They bought their house specifically to accommodate this Stradivarius of pianos.

Richard and Loydeen arrived three days before the wedding. Richard knows and is deeply committed to the virtues of preparing his hands and – equally important – checking out the pianos he's asked to play.

Turns out, to describe this piano as an unmitigated disaster would be a compliment!

Among other things, the piano had not been tuned for decades. It was clearly suffering from a history of having been transported in the back of pickups from one venue to another, including summers at musty old family cottages.

Richard was dismayed but not surprised when he discovered the white key for the note 'A' above middle 'C' would stick down when played. That is, it would go down... and stay down. This meant that during his concert, Richard would get to use that key only once. The joke circulated that Richard would have to decide exactly where during his concert that he most wanted to use that note... just the one time.

Richard concluded that if there were to be a concert, he would have to see about freeing up the sticky key. Now, oil and pianos don't mix, so another remedy was needed. His review of the decrepit upright piano also revealed that one of the three floor pedals was prone to emitting an unconcert-like squawk when pushed down with his foot.

Fortunately, Richard can be quite handy when called upon. After all, a Swiss Army knife is his constant companion. Regardless, he is quite happy to let others repair pianos... he prefers to do the playing. But this time, there no "others" to do the job, so he and his Swiss Army knife went to work.

Off came the front panel under the keyboard. What his eyes feel upon amused and shocked him so much that he called his sister to come have a look. She saw what Richard had discovered... six empty beer cans nestled at the bottom of the piano, one of them wedged beneath a lever activated by the offending pedal, creating that well known beer-can crunch. Seems someone had been dispatching his or her empties through an opening in the back of the piano.

Richard turned his attention next to the sticking 'A' key. He knew the usual cause was the alignment of various shafts and joints connecting the keys to the hammers that strike the strings. Richard began checking all the connections. At first, everything seemed to be in order. Then he looked more closely. Nestled at the base of one connection was a solid gold necklace, owner unknown.

How did it get there? Equally unknown. The problem of the sticking “A” key had been solved.

The concert went on. Richard’s playing was brilliant... his performance extremely well received, as always.

The Bird Dog

We hadn't planned on taking a bird dog along on our pheasant-hunting trip. But we got one just the same... a two-legged version. This is how it happened.

Pheasant hunting was a popular sport when I was a young man. My father was an avid pheasant hunter. We had a tradition – Dad and I hunted together on the first day of the season. One fall, with the hunting season fast approaching, I was explaining this tradition to a colleague at work when he said:

"Hey, that sounds really interesting. Do you think your Dad would mind if I came along?"

Eaton Howitt was a master at self-invitations.

"Have you ever used a shotgun?" I asked.

"Good heavens, no!" Eaton replied. "I've never even held a gun."

We all know that hunting can be a dangerous sport. Most hunters are cautious about who they take along. Eaton was a city guy, through and through. Convincing Dad to let me invite him would be a challenge.

Eaton was an enigma to us young reporters at the daily newspaper where we worked. He was older than us and had come to work for our small daily newspaper in the west from a big eastern company. The career flow usually went in the other direction. Within a few months of his arrival, Eaton surprised us by being promoted to one of the company's more prestigious positions. We found out later he was attempting to make a fresh start after some personal challenges.

Eaton quickly became enamored with the western lifestyle he'd found in his adopted home city. He made friends with prominent ranchers and the descendants of pioneers, recognizing them as sources of anecdotes for the western-style mystery novels he told us he was determined to write one day. So, an abundance of first hand knowledge about life in the country would be essential.

Evidently, he decided that a pheasant-hunting trip fit his criteria. I knew it would be a challenge to convince Dad to let him come along. Eaton wasn't making things any easier. He pestered me for weeks about the hunting trip, asking if I'd talked to Dad yet. I kept assuring him that I would regardless of my apprehension. The problem was, despite Eaton's presumed city virtues, his country acumen was noticeable by its absence. He had never hunted before, nor even held a shotgun, and knew nothing about dressing for a hunting trip or for anything else to do with the outdoors.

Opening day was on a Tuesday. I'd booked that day off work as vacation time.

On the previous Friday my folks had invited me for supper. They lived in a small town a few miles away.

"I've a friend in the office who'd like to go hunting with us," I told Dad over supper that evening. "What do you think?"

"Has he hunted before?" came Dad's predictable reply.

"Well, no," I said. "But I've explained to him how it works and what he must do in order to keep safe."

"Surely he doesn't want to carry a gun?" Dad said.

"Oh no!" I said. "He doesn't even have a hunting license. I'll keep him out of the way. He just wants to see up close what goes on during a pheasant hunt. Do you think that would be all right?"

"Well, all right," Dad said. "But I don't like it. Just remember, you're responsible for him."

On Monday evening, I arrived back at my parents' home in time for supper. I had Eaton in tow. Yeah, the timing was strategic – we were both bachelors. Mom's home cooked meals were culinary treasures to be relished.

Making friends was second nature to Eaton. His unruly mop of dark brown hair and bushy moustache, atop his six-foot 220-pound frame, served to magnify the self-assurance he made no effort to conceal. And his booming voice commanded attention wherever he went.

During supper, Eaton worked his charm. In no time the conversation around the dining room table sounded more like a gathering for old home week than the polite offering of a meal to a stranger.

On Tuesday morning we were up before dawn. Dad had arranged to hunt with a farmer friend who'd posted his land with "No Trespassing" signs all around. The signs kept other hunters away but did not prohibit hunting, as "No Hunting" signs would have done.

Crops that were grown on the farm required irrigation. That meant the all-important irrigation ditches. Pheasants loved to hide in those ditches. Being fall, crops had been harvested for the year. Water was no longer required that season to grow crops. The six-foot-deep ditches were dry. Weeds that blew into the bottoms of the ditches provided excellent hiding places for pheasants.

Eaton appeared to be almost as eager as he was apprehensive.

Hunters normally take turns walking along the bottom of the ditches to flush out pheasants from hiding places. Those walks are unpleasant and unpopular. It means stumbling through waist-deep tumbleweeds with their razor sharp needles. As protection, experienced hunters wore old jeans or heavy coveralls over regular blue jeans. Worst of all, hunters down at the bottom of the ditches seldom got a clear shot at a pheasant.

Wealthier hunters in our area had trained bird dogs they could send down into the ditches. We didn't.

"Where do you want me to be?" Eaton asked as we gathered beside a long irrigation ditch that reached across a big harvested field, the soil prepared for winter.

"Walk along the bottom of the ditch," Dad instructed an unsuspecting Eaton. "From there you'll have a good view of what goes on, and it'll be a lot safer for you. The rest of us will be walking along the top. We'll be on both sides of the ditch. When the pheasants fly up, we'll be shooting. So make absolutely sure that you don't get ahead of us."

Eaton seemed to like the idea of the good view, and he took to heart in particular the advice Dad gave him about staying behind us.

When the hunt ended for the day, Eaton's city-type pant legs were torn in a multitude of places by thorns, his skin was punctured, he had blisters on his feet from the city oxford shoes he'd been wearing, and above all for him he had a story to tell everyone back at the office. But in typical Eaton style, he went one better than that.

He wrote a weekly column for the newspaper that normally was about events in the city. When his next column appeared, it told a harrowing tale with tongue firmly in cheek of how he'd been pressed into service against his will as the world's very first two-legged bird dog.

The Bully

Eddie Vargas was a bully. He was also my age and my neighbor.

It surprised many who met him for the first time, since Eddie was a smaller that average sized kid. It was his vicious temper and eagerness to fight that intimidated other kids, even bigger and older boys.

Eddie lived in a big old house on the edge of our small town... an only child. We'd moved in across the street, one house from the corner, in a brand new subdivision.

I first saw Eddie through an opening in the big trees lining their front yard. The faded yellow clapboard house was on the corner, facing a street that intersected ours. I watched him drop his bike on the front sidewalk and race up the front steps into their screened porch. That was the day after we'd moved into our new house. I was 12 and excited that a boy my own age was living across the street. I hadn't met Eddie, so assumed he attended the Catholic school up the street. My sisters and I were at the public school.

Mom insisted I go across the street and meet Eddie. His mother answered the rickety screen door. Mrs. Vargas was friendly and enthusiastic when I told her we'd just moved in. I was slightly aware her hair was unkept and her voice slurred when she talked. She kept sipping at something in a squat drinking glass and puffing on a cigarette.

I told her I'd come to meet her son. Mrs. Vargas said she didn't think Eddie was home. That's when I learned his name. Her reply surprised me... his bicycle was clearly visible on the sidewalk. Later that evening, I could see Eddie through the scraggly hedge that formed the side fence of their back yard. He was playing alone. Eddie seemed fully occupied. I didn't go over.

A few weeks later, I was passing their house on my way downtown. Mrs. Vargas called from the porch. She came quickly to the front gate. It was obvious she wanted me to make friends with Eddie. I suggested he phone me or come over. She wrote down our phone number. I never heard from him.

I was going to invite Eddie to become a Boy Scout. I'd joined a new troop. The leader was an amazing guy. Les Marriott was a war veteran with a love of the outdoors. He was excited about me sharing with others the skills I'd learned while living on a farm before we moved to town. I realized the other kids didn't know things like tying knots, making a campfire or building a shelter in the woods. It made me feel good to share things that others didn't know.

Eddie and I would encounter each other occasionally on our bicycles, going in opposite directions. He would look my way sometimes, but didn't seem to see me. He never replied when I said 'Hi'. I wanted to be friendly... I'd heard about his reputation.

During the next few years, my circle of friends grew and Eddie was soon forgotten, mostly. I would see him less and less often across the street. We heard occasional rumors about him. Once, we heard he'd been on probation for beating up some kid. He was still living at home but attending a special program for troubled kids.

We were in our late teens when his father's business went bankrupt. Rumors were that Mr. Vargas was an alcoholic, drinking during the day at his car and truck tire business, and then drinking at home with his wife in the evening. The outcome was no surprise.

By that time, most of us were finishing high school and looking forward to the independence that graduation promised. Memories of Eddie had receded to the farther reaches of my mind. And like teenagers, we were all dating or trying to.

Kirby and I had begun dating three years earlier.

We didn't realize it at first, but fellow students envied our ongoing relationship. Her parents were so concerned about it they sent her off to a private school in another city for a year to keep us apart, and presumably 'cool our jets' a tad. When Kirby returned in the spring, we became 'an item' again, showing up on Saturday nights with other teenaged couples at the local hangout, the aging Regal Café.

One Saturday evening in mid-summer we were gathering as usual at the Regal to hang out as teenagers do. I'd found a parking spot for my semi-customized metallic blue Chevy two door, half a block from the café. Kirby and I were just about to enter the café when I heard my name called. I looked up the street and there was Eddie Vargas. I hadn't seen him for a more than a year. His parents had moved out of their house some time earlier.

"Hey, Big Shot!" I heard Eddie say, after calling my name a second time. "Where the f--- do you think you're going?"

"Hi Eddie," I replied, trying to keep my temper in front of Kirby. I knew she had a strong dislike for foul language. "How're ya doing? Haven't seen you for a long time." I was hoping to calm him by at least appearing to be unperturbed. It didn't work.

"I'm not surprised, asshole," he said. He sounded drunk. "What'sa matter? D'ya think you're too ---ing good for the likes of me?" I knew that responding further would serve no useful purpose. He wanted to fight. But being small and light for my age, I was anything but a fighter. Any fight would be one sided and over painfully fast. The few skills I had in that department came from a couple of lessons in boxing and wrestling that our scoutmaster Mr. Marriott had given us. It was shaky stuff against an experienced street fighter like Eddie.

A crowd had begun to gather on the wide sidewalk in front of the Regal. I turned to Kirby and asked her to go inside. She refused, but agreed to step back a few paces into the safety of the crowd of kids just behind me. Those behind Eddie kept a respectful distance well behind him.

He stepped toward me. Without warning, his hands shot up and he pushed me hard in the chest. I stumbled back a few steps. My back bumped into someone in the crowd. I moved forward and quickly stepped sideways, hoping to dodge his next move. My back was toward the café. Eddie had circled in the opposite direction. His back was to a car parked at the curb.

Slowly, his right foot braced his weight on the bumper. And then he lunged at me, his right fist coming up. Instinctively, or perhaps desperately, I thought of a wrestling move that Mr. Marriott had taught us in Scouts. Much to Eddie's surprise, I stepped toward him and grabbed the lapels of his jacket. Then I stepped back quickly, falling backward. Eddie was startled when he felt my weight propelling him forward.

Like Mr. Marriott had taught us, as I was falling backward toward sidewalk I raised my right foot up to Eddie's stomach. I pushed hard, firmly holding his jacket at first, and then letting go has he was propelled over me. Until then, I hadn't thought about what was behind me. I was thinking how bad it would look for me to lose a fight in front of my girlfriend and our friends.

My plan was that I would flip Eddie so he would hit the cement sidewalk on his back, hurting him enough to discourage him from fighting. The maneuver had worked that way in practice at the Scout hall on tumbling mats. But I must have released Eddie's jacket too soon. Instead of flipping over, he went sailing head first behind me.

The Regal Café had a huge plate glass window bearing its name, painted in a crescent shape. It was directly behind me. I'd forgotten. Eddie went sailing head first through the window. He landed on his stomach on the wide bench-like windowsill, his head up against the back of the Wurlitzer record player. The clothes on his back and the three-foot wide windowsill were covered in razor-like shards of broken glass. Eddie was stunned at first. So was I. But I was pleased I'd got the best of him, if only briefly.

I looked around for Kirby and began to plot our escape. The crowds cheered. Eddie rolled over. Apprehension swept through me. Small cuts on his face oozed blood. I wondered what he'd do next. Unexpectedly, his eyes grew wide in fear. I was secretly proud of that, too, until I looked up.

Eddie was focused on a long, sharp pointed wedge of glass hanging above him from the top edge of the window, poised directly over his stomach. It could fall at any moment, joining the other broken glass. It was so big and sharp that if it fell there was no doubt it would pierce his stomach, perhaps even go right through him.

Oh my God! I thought. The crowd saw it too. They grew silent.

Eddie uttered strange guttural whimpering sounds deep in his throat as he carefully worked his way sideways, keeping his terror-filled eyes on the dangling wedge of glass. Then he gingerly wiggled, feet first, out the window. No one offered to help. Eddie fell to his knees on the sidewalk. He paused for a few seconds, wiping blood from his face with his right hand. Then he stood, and without looking at anyone, walked away in the direction he'd come.

I never saw Eddie again.

Two 'Spirited' Boys

My friend Mike and I were equally to blame. We were eight years old. He got just as drunk as me, I think. My memory's kinda fuzzy.

We learned a lesson or two that day.

The scene of the crime was a big country wedding. Two days of it... or so they told us later. Mike's cousin had married a pretty girl from down the road. The first day of celebrations was at the bride's family home, right after the ceremony. The second day was at the groom's family farm. Mike and I made it to the first day; we didn't make the second. We were grounded.

The parents of both the bride and the groom had moved to Canada many years earlier from Eastern Europe. Everyone lived modestly on marginal farms, including us, but they knew how to party with enthusiasm, whenever there was a good reason. A wedding was as a very good reason.

Nancy and Sidney's wedding was the first party to come along in a long time. It was mid-July... a good time of year... long after spring farm work, and a few weeks before the first crops would be harvested and preserved for winter.

The first day of partying was at the bride's home. It was a perfect setting, overlooking a deep wide valley and a meandering creek. Only the neighbor women doing the cooking could go into the house. Mike's mother and my mother were among them. Oh, and Nancy's father was allowed in – he was in charge of the booze stored there.

The celebration began with more than two hours of music mixed with an abundant flow of spirits. Polkas and foxtrots mingled freely with beer, wine, whiskey, vodka and lots of home brew. Tables, chairs and benches covered the lawn.

Then it was dinnertime. Huge platters piled a foot high with meat, and massive bowls of vegetables crowded the tables, vying for space with an amazing range of homegrown treats and condiments. Hungry guests occupied every available place on the chairs and benches arranged around or along both sides of long tables.

Food occupied so much space on the tables there was barely room for half-empty wine or liquor glasses or beer bottles. None of the guests wanted to relinquish their drinks. They found or created reasonably level places on the lawn beneath where they were seated.

This all happened more than half a century ago, when eight year olds were noticed occasionally at social events, but mostly they were ignored as long as they stayed out of trouble. All children of that day recall hearing the demeaning admonition: “children should be seen and not heard”. It was good to be not seen. Too much visibility usually resulted in unwelcome errands or chores.

This day, it was easy for Mike and I to be invisible; our parents and the other adults were preoccupied with the merriment. First we sat on the grass in the shade of the tables and guests. It was a very hot day. Soon, we were crawling on the cool grass in the shade of the chairs and benches. I went down one side, Mike the other, at first playing some made up game. It wasn't long before both of us were sipping away on the glasses we were crawling past, most of them half full. Hey, it was a hot day and we were thirsty.

I didn’t like the taste of beer. Mike was okay with it. But the wine tasted really good, especially the red stuff. And there were lots of glasses containing Coke and ginger ale... mixed with something else that made them smell funny. Hey, remember... cold and wet are antidotes for heat. That’s good, right?

At first, we took just little sips from the glasses. We didn’t want the owners to know some of their drink had gone AWOL. That changed after we crawled over to the next group of tables. For some reason we were feeling much bolder.

Maybe it was all the exertion – from our game and from trying not to laugh and draw attention. The more we crawled the more and more generous we became for ourselves with the adults' parked drinks.

But finally, the inevitable happened. Someone caught us. Promptly, we were dispatched on an errand to get something from a cold storage enclosure down the hill. The farm home was perched on the edge of the deep valley. A creek wandered along the valley floor below. The cold storage box was in a spring that flowed into the creek. It was a steep walk down the hill to the spring and a long hike back up... even at the best of times.

Mike and I made it down, all right. We rolled and laughed most of the way. Getting back up was another matter. We had to walk. There was just one problem. The earth kept coming up and hitting us in the face. And we couldn't stop laughing.

I don't remember whether we made it up the hill to the house with whatever it was we'd been sent to get. It's very doubtful. But somehow, Mike and I must have got to the top of the hill. Well, I think so, 'cause someone apparently saw our odd behavior and told our parents.

I remember seeing Mike's shirt collar being grabbed by his tall, husky Dad. Mike's feet barely touched the ground as he was led away. Just about then, Mom grabbed my upper left arm in the vice grip of her amazingly strong right hand. That was her 'official' disciplinary hold when I'd done something she disapproved of. The frequency in recent years had made that grip familiar.

Both Mike and I were hustled away from the wedding festivities... and from the view of chuckling guests... toward the road and the parked cars. Mike's family lived 1½ miles away in one direction. He was dumped unceremoniously in the back of his Dad's pick-up. He was lying on his back laughing away as the pickup disappeared in a cloud of dust.

My family lived ½ mile away in the other direction. Mom wasn't about to wait for Dad to get the car. I recall being propelled down the gravel road, stumbling and falling quite often, listening to my thoroughly humiliated mother vent in tones that increased in volume the farther we got from the wedding celebration.

I'm not quite sure, but some of the alcohol I consumed must have come back up the way it went down, along with the snacks we'd scavenged. Perhaps that's why Mom threw a few buckets of ice-cold well water down the front of my clothes. I was ordered to disrobe in the back yard and then hang my shirt and pants on the clothesline.

The sun wasn't down, but Mom decreed it was bedtime for me. I didn't object, being pretty well out of it.

Our home had two stories. The bedrooms were on the second floor. There was a very long enclosed staircase, straight up. My room was at the top, across the hall.

To appreciate fully what happened next, it's important to understand everything that was located at the bottom of those stairs. From the kitchen, you walked up three steps to a door. Behind it was a small landing, and then you turned 90 degrees to go up the long flight of stairs. Our coats, hats and mitts went onto hooks along two sides of the landing. Shoes, rubber boots and winter boots all went on the floor under the coats.

Oh, yes, and there was a thunder bucket... a white enamel potty. The lip and the edge of the lid were decorated with a blue pinstripe. There's a reason for having such a detailed knowledge. Tell ya in a minute.

The role of the thunder bucket was the usual – it saved family members from trekking out at night and in winter to the outhouse, located on the far side of our back yard. The potty didn't get emptied every day. It was supposed to. But in fact, several days might go by occasionally... it could get quite full. And yes, the distraction of the wedding excitement precipitated one of those 'quite full' days.

So there I was, lying in bed, hanging onto the edges trying to keep it from spinning and swaying. I decided just then that I needed to pee. But I was still unsteady on my feet. It was still daylight. I started down the stairs heading for the outhouse. I didn't make it.

At the top of the stairs, my balance deserted me. I remember catapulting down, coming to rest with my face buried in my big sister's coat hanging at the bottom of the stairs. My right hand was buried in someone's rubber boot and then my left hand went splashing into the thunder bucket with its nearly full contents... an obnoxiously odorous mixture of both 'numbers'.

By this time, the rest of my thoroughly humiliated family had made their way home. They were seated at the kitchen table, no doubt consoling one another when their only son, one hand caught in the handle of the thunder bucket, rolled out of the stairwell landing and onto the kitchen floor.

It seemed like hours before I got that mess cleaned up... all by myself. Mom supervised the mopping up with an old towel, the hand wringing into buckets, the washing, the rinsing and the drying of floor. Dad made sure the thunder bucket was scrubbed and washed yet again, and then polished and shined with car wax until it was clean and sparkling, inside and out.

Evidently, Mike's experience was a bit different... but no less instructive.

For the next few days I observed that he rode his bike standing up, and was mighty uncomfortable while sitting at his desk beside me in school. He'd jump to his feet the moment recess was called, and volunteered for blackboard duty a lot. It wasn't like him... but he got over it quickly.

Tommy's Tool Kit

For some people, Christmas generates unpredictable side effects. And for young Tommy, his Christmas turned out to be one of those.

Like most boys, Tommy was attracted to things mechanical. Maybe it's in their DNA. But Tommy had a disadvantage – there were no male influences in his house, at first.

Tommy's mom was a single parent. He was born two weeks after his father died of leukemia. He became the youngest of seven children... and the only boy. Now that's a challenge.

A change came into Tommy's life soon after he turned six years old. His oldest sister, Susan, announced to the family that she'd invited someone to dinner on the weekend. A few months earlier, she'd started a job in the city, 30 miles from the small town where they lived. Her guest was a co-worker.

As it turned out Susan's guest Matt was handy with tools and enjoyed fixing things. Susan's mother, Ester, was delighted. A long list of things in her 100+-year-old two-story house needed repair. Ester had been a widow for more than six years. She was remarkably clever in many ways, but home repairs were not her forte. Matt showed up the next weekend with a tool kit and went to work. Tommy followed Matt everywhere... up the back stairs and down the front stairs, throughout the house, into the basement, and around outside. For the next few weekends, Tommy could have been Matt's shadow.

Matt and Susan had been dating for a few months when they arrived at her Mother's house for Christmas. Among their gifts for each member of the family was a very special gift for Tommy – a pint-sized tool kit. It had everything: hammer, screwdriver, ruler, level, and tape measure... it even had a small but real saw.

Tommy was more than overjoyed. Ester was impressed. Tommy saw Matt as a role model. Ester was pleased her son had a male influence. Ester's brother-in-law, Jack, worked full time in the city and was farming nearby, as well. He had little time to spend one-on-one with Tommy. Ester's big fear was that Matt would 'disappear', that is, if Matt and Susan were to break up. She knew it would devastate Tommy.

By then, Susan and Matt had been romantically involved for more than six months. Ester was not one to mince words, so she explained her fears to Matt. She needn't have been concerned. Unbeknown to both, Susan had already decided she was going to marry Matt. It's just that... well... she hadn't told her mother yet... or even Matt.

Tommy's toolbox went everywhere with him. He would place it carefully beside the tub during his baths. He even took it to bed. Ester insisted that when Tommy went to school the tool kit had to stay behind. It was the first thing he looked for when he got home. And when Matt came to visit on the weekends, Tommy would quickly grab his toolkit, and accompany Matt while he fixed doorknobs, dripping water taps, slow drains, sticky kitchen cupboard doors, stubborn hinges, drafty windows, sagging verandahs, loose floorboards, holes in the walls, creaky stairs, broken clotheslines, and a seemingly endless list of other odd jobs.

Not long after New Year's, Matt and Susan arrived as usual at her mother's home for a weekend visit. The excitement that normally accompanied their arrival was missing. Susan's siblings were nowhere to be seen. Matt and Susan found out later they were cowering out of sight in the living room. When they walked through the back door, Ester was in the kitchen, hands in the sink, her back to them. When she heard the door close, Ester lifted her apron and wiped her hands as she turned and looked at them. Her face wore a stern look.

"Is anything wrong?" Susan asked, glancing back

and forth between her Mother and Matt. She was surprised her Mother hadn't walked over and given her a big hug, as she usually did. Her normally reserved mother had even started giving Matt hugs, too. Not this time.

"Is anything wrong?" Ester replied firmly, her tiny body almost rigid. "I should think so!" she added, her tone of voice rising.

Ester walked over to the kitchen table. Her late husband had built it for the family while being treated for leukemia. The table was partly obscured by a large vinyl tablecloth that hung down on all sides.

Ester reached down and lifted the corner of the tablecloth nearest her. That was where she sat. Before Susan got her job and moved to the city, she would sit at the other end, being the eldest. They kept peace among the six other children during meals.

"What do you think of that?" Ester demanded, glancing down at the table leg beside her. The table's endplates at both ends had been fashioned from single sheets of heavy plywood and also formed the legs. They were attached to the tabletop, itself cut from a full sheet of sturdy plywood.

The leg on the other side of the table rested firmly on the floor, as intended. The leg closest to her was propped up on a three-inch pile of books. Matt could see that even with the books the table was still uneven.

"Your tools," Ester said, pointing accusingly with her other hand. "Your tools did that!"

Turns out Ester had complained earlier that week at supper about the table being uneven. Tommy took it upon himself to fix the problem. But instead of shimming up the short leg, he decided, when no one was looking, to shorten the 'long' leg.

Ester was beyond annoyed with the damage to the table that Tommy's father had lovingly built for his family just months before he died. She held Matt and Susan fully responsible. After all, they'd bought the handsaw that Tommy had used. And she challenged Matt to fix "this disaster".

The next morning, Matt and Tommy visited a local lumberyard and found a sturdy piece of surplus plywood. At home, with Tommy holding the piece firmly on a box in the back yard, Matt trimmed the piece to match the shape of the errant leg. He used Tommy's little saw. Tommy was pleased about that.

They went back inside and clamped the piece of wood to the leg. Then, Matt used a drill from his own toolbox to make pilot holes, and inserted screws, securing the repair piece in place. Problem solved.

For years thereafter, Ester and her daughters got considerable 'mileage' from recounting that story to anyone who'd listen to, 'The Saga of Tommy's Toolkit'.

Kicking The Habit

Sister Ella Zink was a conventional nun, at first... but with a decidedly unconventional future. In the 1970s, she was a pioneer, often venturing far outside the conventions of life in a convent that were prevalent at that time.

Her early career had been traditional. She served as a medical nurse in remote communities for several decades. Then, she began kicking over the traces by becoming a professional public relations practitioner for the Roman Catholic Church.

PR was an uncommon field for women at the time, even more so for for a nun. That bothered her not in the slightest. In fact, she relished the job, bringing to her work a wit and charm, and an enthusiasm that infected everyone around her. That was no easy task – her bosses were a group of dour and staunchly traditional Roman Catholic bishops.

Sister Ella's short and stocky build presented an imposing figure as she bustled about press conferences and other public events, resplendent in a nun's habit of flowing grey robes and hood trimmed in white.

Characteristically, Sister Ella felt called also to serve others outside her main work. Many young aspiring PR practitioners learned how to become better in their chosen field thanks to her. It was logical that she'd become involved with the national public relations society and its programs to develop and accredit PR practitioners.

In due course, Ella was appointed to chair the national accreditation board. She became an icon of professional standards and moral integrity for all who practiced the profession. Ella was a PR natural. She was blessed with a charismatic personality and a brilliant smile that lit up a room when she entered. Someone once described her as "an animated fire hydrant with a heart of gold". Upon hearing that characterization for the first time, she reacted with an ebullient – and decidedly unladylike – belly laugh that started somewhere around her well tended 'sensible' shoes and gained momentum upward until it erupted forth, engulfing all around with her infectious laugh. Despite her charm, few had the nerve to argue with Ella and her high standards... she could impose with zeal her abundant intellect and sharp tongue upon deserving miscreants.

As accreditation chair, her duties included recruiting new board members to fill vacancies. New appointees were welcomed at the board's annual meeting each year.

One year, the board had only one new member. The young appointee had worked in PR for only six years. He'd received his professional designation a year prior to this appointment. The prestigious appointment to the accreditation board had left him surprised, flattered and apprehensive.

While riding down the elevator to his very first accreditation board meeting, he was in awe of the legendary Sister Ella Zink, BSc, BSW, RN, APR, whom he assumed (correctly) was responsible for his appointment. They'd spoken on the phone often about professional matters but had never met.

Not surprising, he'd slept fitfully, arriving at the meeting room 15 minutes early.

The door was open. He stepped into the room. It appeared empty. An urn of fresh coffee was to his left. He began walking toward it. He lit his first cigarette of the day, criticizing himself for his many failed attempts at quitting. At the time, smoking was still permitted in public areas although the anti-smoking juggernaut was gaining momentum rapidly.

"I take mine black," a robust female voice said off to his right. The unexpected voice startled him. He turned and saw a figure butting out a cigarette. All he could make out was a vague outline of a stocky figure framed in the light of the window behind her. The morning light created a halo effect. He recalled later how appropriate that was.

The young man poured two cups of black coffee and walked toward the window. The woman stepped forward. She accepted a cup with her left hand, offering her right. He got a good look at the short robust figure in front of him.

The stout middle-aged woman wore a light greyish pink, stylishly tailored woman's business suit. He guessed she was a lawyer, accountant or business executive. His mind's eye scrolled unsuccessfully through the list of other board members. No match.

Must be someone else, he thought, wondering if he was in the wrong room. He prepared to introduce himself. Then he heard:

"Hi, I'm Ella Zink."

The young man was taken aback, his mouth open and wordless. What he saw before him was not what the legends had led him to expect. Recognizing the young man's surprise, Sister Ella's kindly eyes shone mischievously. She smiled broadly, and then promptly filled the void of his unasked question:

"Oh, I kicked the habit!"

For years thereafter, Ella would be introduced often, and with much affection by her legions of friends and colleagues as "the nun who kicked the habit".

The Gold Boulder

We all know legends grow with the retelling. This one's about a gold boulder and how it caused a murder. Or did it? We're not sure. But that won't stop us from telling you what we think we know.

The question is... did a boulder of gold really slip from the hands of a murderer and roll down a mountainside, and then disappear into a deep lake?

In the late 1800s, prospectors were scouring mountains for gold and other precious metals in the western US and Canada. A few struck it rich, and some were murdered, their riches stolen. Most left empty handed.

This legend – or legends – began on Kootenay Lake in British Columbia, Canada.

One version is full of intrigue, betrayal and murder. Another is much less sensational but more likely to be true. Perhaps. Chances are, we'll never know.

Let's begin with the sensational version. It's much more fun.

It tells of a prospector working his claim on a mountain stream a few hundred feet above Kootenay Lake coming upon traces of gold. Developing the site became a bigger job than he expected. So he returned to a nearby settlement, to spend time with his wife, and to look for help. He found an experienced miner, took him home and the two made plans to develop the prospector's claim. He didn't know that in his absence his attractive young wife and the miner had already become, shall we say, familiar.

The men trekked back to the claim and went to work. The prospector promised the miner a share of all the gold they found. Their work was rewarded with an abundance of gold flakes and small nuggets.

Spurred on, they worked feverously to convert the claim into a mine. Lo' and behold they uncovered an outcropping of gold. After days of hard work, the outcropping proved to be a boulder, apparently of solid gold.

This version of the legend is unclear about the size of the boulder. Suffice to say, it was so large that together they were barely able to move it. They decided to lower their discovery down the mountainside, using ropes and pulleys attached to sturdy trees, to the lakeshore where their boat was moored. The two built a scaffold on shore to lift the boulder into the boat. From there, they'd transport it to a buyer and collect their fortune.

Construction of the scaffold took longer than expected... the work being interrupted frequently by drunken celebrations and hangovers. Meanwhile, the boulder remained where they'd found it. The miner couldn't get the hugely valuable gold boulder out of his mind, nor for that matter, the prospector's attractive wife. One drunken evening an argument broke out about the prospector's wife. A fight ensued. The miner is said to have grabbed a rifle and shot the prospector.

The miner decided to make a run for it. But he didn't want to leave the gold boulder behind, nor the newly created widow. He decided to enlist gravity to move the mammoth nugget, by rolling it down the mountain to the shore. However, he overlooked one important detail: how to stop the boulder when it reached the shore. Down it went through the forest, gaining momentum along the way. It bounced onto the rocky shore and with a mighty splash, rolled into the lake. Some say it's 500 feet deep there.

The legend says the miner sought to persuade the prospector's wife to accompany him. Turns out he would have fled not only empty-handed but alone. Before he could get away someone turned him in. Rumors say it was the prospector's wife, now the owner of a prosperous gold mine. The miner was arrested, tried and hanged.

The other version has the best claim to legitimacy. It's based upon a story about it that first appeared in a local newspaper. It credits discovery of the gold boulder to a man out searching for lost cattle.

The story said a man named Randal Kemp found the famous boulder while he and three others were searching a bay on Kootenay Lake for the cattle. They pulled into shore for a rest. Kemp sat down and leaned against a large boulder. He idly poked at it with a prospector's axe he was carrying. The axe kept sticking in the 'rock'. After clearing away overburden, the four men were startled to discover the rock was almost solid gold.

The four took samples, and measurements. The legend says it measured 27 inches long, 14 inches deep and 12 inches wide. They determined a boulder that size would weigh 48,000 ounces. At 2015 prices of about $1,200 an ounce the boulder would be worth about $57.6 million. Little wonder hundreds have attempted to find the boulder.

The four men developed a plan to retrieve their find. They would lower the boulder into a sturdy boat and take it to a local community where they would sell it. One end of an inch-thick rope was fashioned into a sling and placed around the two-ton boulder. Two skids were built and the boulder rolled onto them. They would lower the boulder, using the skids and pulleys attached to trees, down the slope and into the boat.

At first, everything went as planned. But the weight proved too much for the rope. It broke. The unfettered boulder bounced down the mountainside, over a cliff and landed on the boat, reducing it to rubble. The boulder rolled down a steep underwater incline into the depths. Recovery of the boulder was not possible. No one knew the depth of the lake. Guesses ranged from 400 to over a thousand feet.

Many have visited the lake in search of the infamous gold boulder. So far, no one has proven or disproven the existence of the gold boulder. So the searches... and the legends... go on.

Acknowledgements

Most of the stories in this collection are based upon, or were inspired by, real people or real events. My gratitude to everyone that in some way played a role in the creation of one or more of these stories. I trust that as they read through Encounters With Life*, these fine people will see and enjoy their contributions and in so doing feel my deep gratitude coming through to each of them.*

Sincere thanks and congratulations to Solstice Publishing for having the courage and the consummate skills to become leaders in the meteoric rise of the independent publishing industry. The middle ground in the book industry between the shrinking role of traditional publishers and the ever-present vanity publishers has grown exponentially due in large measure to Solstice and like-minded publishers. My special thanks go to Solstice CEO Melissa Miller for her exceptional support and guidance in the preparation of this collection.

Above all, I am especially grateful to my wonderful wife Sharolie Osborne for her encouragement and for her patience. Writing may be a solitary endeavor, but it becomes that also for those closest to the writer. Without her ongoing encouragement to seek publication for these short stories, it is unlikely this collection ever would have happened.

James Osborne

14167203R00097

Made in the USA
Middletown, DE
18 November 2018